DOG
EARS

ANNE BOOTH

Catnip
PUBLISHING LTD

To Helen Neame
Thank you for listening.

CATNIP BOOKS
Published by Catnip Publishing Ltd
320 City Road
London EC1V 2NZ
www.catnippublishing.co.uk

This edition first published 2015

3 5 7 9 10 8 6 4 2

ISBN 978-1-84647-188-9

Printed in India by Replika Press Pvt. Ltd.

www.catnippublishing.co.uk

Monday

Chapter One

It's nice having breakfast with you, Timmy, even if you do slurp yours down too fast. And then eye up my toast when I'm eating mine.

But yes, you're sitting really well, even though I didn't actually ask you to. And I wish you wouldn't keep drooling. It's a bit off-putting. Here – have one of your biscuits if you're still hungry. They're better for you than toast.

Good boy.

I need to find my pencil case and my planner. I've decided I'm coming back from the break MUCH more organised. This is a new me. A New Anna Taylor. Can you believe I've been in Year 7 for a whole half term now? St Faith's seems like fifty million years ago.

Remember Year 6, Tim?

You were brilliant when I was worried that

Emma liked the new girl Mohona more than me.

And then when I thought I might like Mohona more than Emma. Because she was really nice and she wanted to come to tea and visit Mum's shop. And she wasn't as bossy as Emma.

And when Emma cried about it.

Which was awful. Emma never cries.

And then when Emma, Mohona and I decided we were all best friends forever and three is a perfect number for a girl gang.

You didn't panic. You knew it was going to be okay.

I can't imagine it not being the three of us. Emma and Mohona are the best friends ever.

The best human friends, of course. Don't look at me like that with your big brown eyes. Hey – I'd better hurry up and make my sandwiches or I'll be late for school. Don't eat that envelope! I know it's junk mail, but that doesn't mean you can chew it. Or is junk mail like junk food for dogs?

Remember when the letter about secondary school came last year, Timmy? I got to the mat just before you grabbed it. Dad told Gran that if it arrived when he was at the hospital with Mum then I didn't have to wait to open it. And it said *Bekesbourne High* and it was so good to have you to hug. Because Gran isn't really a hugger. Do you remember – we did this mad dance in the kitchen and you got really excited and knocked a mug off the side and it broke? Gran got a bit cross but I swept up the pieces and then I rang Emma and Mohona to make sure they were going there too. But I told you first.

Hey – get out of the fridge.

I told you when Mum was rushed into hospital early to have Jack, and you stayed with me when Gran came over.

I told you when Gran said Jack had been born. You wagged your tail so much. We were so happy. Our summer holiday baby. He wasn't even supposed to come until the middle of September. He came just after my birthday. So he was nearly my birthday present. My baby brother. Though I'm glad I got my new phone as well!

I told you when I came back from the hospital after seeing Jack. I told you how tiny he was and how many tubes and wires there were on him in his little glass box, and how I didn't really know what to feel. He was tiny, like you when you were a puppy, Tim, but he wasn't sweet at all.

You were the only one I told that to.

You wiggled your eyebrows and let me hug you and you didn't tell me I was a horrible sister and I shouldn't think that about my baby brother.

And I told you about my first day at Bekesbourne High and getting the bus and how I nearly got the wrong one home until Mohona noticed and yelled 'Anna – get off the bus!' and I had to run down the stairs really quickly and I nearly dropped my bag and the driver shouted 'Make up your mind, girly!' and it was all REALLY EMBARRASSING.

Okay. I know what that nudge means. You can have a bit of cheese. Not too much, though. Sit properly. Don't bounce.

We should have called you Tigger.

I need to get the Sellotape and get your dog hair off my jumper. It's the one I was wearing before the holidays, but it's the only one that's out. Mum must be doing the washing today.

Oh no – look at my tights. They're AWFUL. Dog hair all over them. And now a ladder too.

I told you about Emma's AMAZING discovery that if you freeze your tights before you wear them, they don't ladder as much. You have to defrost them first, obviously. She read it on this website her cousin told her about.

She says it really works.

Though she doesn't have a mad dog jumping up at her for cheese

I hope you haven't run off with the hairbrush again.

Did I tell you Mohona read on the internet about putting bicarbonate of soda in your hair if it is greasy?

I haven't tried that yet, but I'm going to. Gran probably has bicarbonate of soda. I'll ask her.

Why do bananas go black so quickly, Tim? I'll just have to skip fruit today. You don't eat fruit and you're fine. You don't even have to wear clothes. You're so lucky. I wish my uniform fitted better. Or I could just wear a big golden onesie to school.

I'll tell that to Dad later on Skype. He'll laugh. I know, I'll draw him a picture.

You and me have got to look after Mum and Jack for Dad while he is away.

'Anna, Anna – could you come and sit with Jack for a moment?'

Mum is calling. I have to go. Look after Mum. See you after school.

Chapter Two

Down, Timmy! SIT! Good boy. Come on. I'm glad to see you too and I'll take you out soon, but I've got to eat something. Okay, yes, I don't see why you can't share a bit of my sandwich. Here you go. I didn't have time to finish my lunch because we were so busy planning for the most amazing thing ever. This has been a fantastic Monday!

I've got to tell someone, and you're the best listener there is. Mum is asleep with Jack upstairs and Gran hasn't arrived yet, and even if she had, you know that Gran never listens anyway.

Basically, the whole school has gone mad.

'I've just met Mr Parsons in the corridor and he played me a tune on his tie,' said Mohona, looking shocked as she came and sat next to me for morning registration. 'I didn't know what to do.'

'What tune was it?' said Emma from behind us.

The place next to her was empty as usual. Lauren is hardly ever on time, when she does come in, and then she hardly ever talks. It's so annoying. We wish we could just sit in a three, like at primary school. I'm lucky they put me with Mohona for form period, but poor Emma is stuck with Lauren. She didn't go to our primary school so Emma doesn't know her AT ALL.

'I think it was from James Bond,' said Mohona.

'He played that one to me,' said Emma. 'Did he pretend to have a gun and say "Mr Parsons – Licensed to Teach"?'

'No.'

'You're lucky, then.'

'Mr Parsons has another really cool tie with a Tardis. It plays the Doctor Who theme,' said Rhys Thomas, interrupting from across the aisle.

'Yeah, and tomorrow he says he is going to wear his Star Wars one,' said Adam Clark next to him.

Emma rolled her eyes.

Though I actually think a Tardis tie sounds okay.

Lauren arrived and sat down next to Emma, not talking to anyone as usual. Emma pulled a face at us. Poor Emma. Lauren must be the most boring person at Bekesbourne High.

Mrs Berlinski took the register and rushed us off to the hall. She seemed really excited, and she was wearing lipstick, which she normally only does at school concerts.

At assembly Mr Parsons bounded on to the stage. His shirt was very pink and his shoes were EXTREMELY shiny. I don't think I've ever noticed them being that shiny before. Gran would have been very impressed. She's always going on about how people don't polish their shoes enough.

'Good morning, Bekesbourne High!' boomed Mr Parsons. Emma says he always sounds like he is at some rock concert. I quite like it. 'Welcome back! I trust you had a good half-term? And you return to some very exciting news! As you know, the international pop star Frankie Santoro is one of our old girls. Now, Frankie is launching a new charity. She's recording a fundraising song and the big news is . . . she wants *our* school to get involved!'

You could hear 'wows' all over the hall. Even the teachers looked interested.

Frankie Santoro! I can't believe it, Timmy. You're right to wag your tail. Frankie went to Bekesbourne High. She used to go out with Matt from Mum's shop, and she was always coming in to buy vintage clothes there. Do you remember when we saw her on TV wearing them, and Gran said she couldn't understand why a pop star wanted to wear old clothes, and Dad said it would be great publicity for the shop and Mum should write and ask Frankie to mention Buttons and Bows when she was on TV, and Mum got upset and stressed with them both? That was just before Jack was born.

Anyway. Then Mr Parsons said, 'I'm going to let Kaz Baker, who is a television producer, tell you more . . .'

At the words 'television producer' you could feel the excitement mount. Even the teachers sat up straighter.

A woman with long earrings and a scarf smiled at Mr Parsons and stepped forward to talk into a microphone.

'Thank you. We are very excited about Frankie's new charity, which is going to fund music projects for young people, and I want to thank your Head, Mr Parsons, for being so very welcoming and helpful.'

Mr Parsons beamed. If he had looked any more welcoming and helpful he would have burst!

'Frankie has often said how important her school was to her,' continued Kaz Baker, 'and so we thought that it would be fun to film her launching her charity here. We'd like to film the school choir and interview students from across the school, but we've also got a special thing we need to ask. We're going to film Frankie singing her new single – and she wants to be supported by a band from her old school.'

We all got a bit excited, and the teachers had to do some shushing before Kaz Baker could go on. She looked very calm, though. She just waited until we were quiet, smiled and continued.

'We'll be doing the auditions all day next Thursday and will narrow it down to two bands – then when Frankie comes to launch the charity on Friday she will pick the winner. Mr Parsons has also agreed that we can come film the auditions on Thursday and do some interviews – we'll try to meet as many of you as possible!'

Mr Parsons walked up next to her at the microphone, took it from its stand and started striding around the stage. Kaz Baker sat down. There wasn't much else she could do, to be honest. Matt told us that when he and Frankie were at school, Mr Parsons used to do Elvis Presley impressions every Christmas. I thought he might do one then. It was like he had forgotten he was a head teacher and thought he was a pop star. It was so embarrassing.

'Thank you, Mrs Baker. Now, students, a world-class pop star is going to be here, in our midst, and we've got just under two weeks to prepare. So let's show the world how creative and talented ALL Bekesbourne High students are!'

Everyone clapped and drummed their feet for ages. Mr Parsons came back and sat next to Kaz Baker and there was a lot of smiling and nodding going on between them. She didn't seem to be put off by him being a bit weird. The teachers were still shushing as we left the hall, but you could tell they were pretty pleased too.

'I bet that's why he is wearing those ties. He just wants to be on TV,' said Emma as we walked down the corridor after assembly. She's very clever.

'So do I,' said Mohona. She's very honest.

'Me too,' I said.

In maths we noticed that Mr Hawkins had put quite a lot of gel in his hair and was looking very cheered up. He let us have five minutes to talk about Frankie Santoro and then he made us work. I hope he gets on TV. He's always nice, even to Lauren –

most of the teachers get cross with her because she can't be bothered to do their homework.

Mr Peterson gave us LOADS of homework and didn't want to talk about Frankie Santoro AT ALL. He seemed to think that him setting up an inter-form physics challenge was the most exciting thing that has ever happened to this school. Mr Peterson is really strange.

And then it was break, and time for an emergency 'how to get the TV people to notice us' meeting.

'They'll only interview really special pupils across the school,' said Mohona. 'It's not like we can do breakdancing or anything.'

We looked at each other.

'No – we'd never learn in time,' said Emma.

'I bet Jed Reubens will be doing his card tricks,' I said.

He's in Year 10, Timmy, and someone said he is going to be in the Magic Circle or something. Anyway, he's really good at magic, so we couldn't compete.

'Well, we're in the choir,' said Mohona. 'They're definitely going to listen to the choir.'

'But we won't stand out. We're just going to have to form a band and audition,' Emma said. 'It can't be that hard. Suzi Lyons has got one.'

'That's a good idea,' I said. 'You can play guitar, Emma. I can do violin and Mohona can sing.'

'I couldn't sing on my own, you'd have to sing with me,' said Mohona.

So I wrote down:

1. Form a band.
2. Learn how to play violin and sing at same time. (Anna)

Typically, Suzi Lyons overheard our plans.

'You're not thinking of auditioning are you?' she said, coming up to our desk. 'You haven't got a chance. Caitlin and Tanesha and I formed our band practically as soon as we started Year 7.'

It's true. Every lunchtime Suzi sits in the music room and plays piano really loudly and she and Caitlin and Tanesha sing whatever is the latest big hit. I'd like to say they're rubbish but they're not. They are annoyingly good. They've always been like that – even at St Faith's they always got the best parts in things.

But they sort of use up all the air in a room.

'You're only doing it to be on TV,' said Suzi.

That was also true, but Emma didn't let that bother her.

'So you're doing it purely for the love of music, then?' said Emma, glaring at her. 'You can't just ban anyone else from forming a band.'

True again. Rishi and Sam were already playing air guitars in the corner.

'You'll be rubbish, anyway,' said Suzi, which was mean AND untrue, so that made our true bit slightly better than hers. She stomped off to find Caitlin and Tanesha.

Emma says she already knows three chords on guitar and thinks she can learn a couple more by the time the film crew come. I can play the violin a little bit now. I've been learning since the start of Year 7, which is practically two months. Miss Green said in my lesson today that if I practised I could be good.

So the plan is we will sound amazing and we will win the competition.

I really want this term to go well. First of all, I've already sorted out the ingredients for food tech on Wednesday. I don't want another situation like the fish pie.

'*Anna, I'm so sorry. I've been so busy. Tell them what's been happening at home. They'll understand.*'

'What do you mean, you forgot the *fish*?' Mrs White said. 'It's not exactly difficult. You've remembered the flour and margarine. What did you think we were making – air pie?'

It was awful, Tim. Everyone laughed.

I hate Mrs White.

Mohona said I could have some of her fish, and Mrs White said, 'That's very good of you, Mohona, are you sure? It hardly seems fair that you should have less fish in *your* pie because someone else can't be bothered to remember the obvious.'

Which was true. But Mohona did have an awful lot of fish.

'Mum always gives me too much. I'm glad I can share it. And I don't like fish pie anyway,' said Mohona.

Thank goodness for Mohona.

Chapter Three

Do dogs have grandmothers? I suppose you must, Tim. But I bet your gran wouldn't take over the way mine does.

I'm so sorry she made you leave the dining room this evening. It's just she's got a thing about dog hair and babies, and you do moult loads. If I had time I could knit a jumper just from your hair. Frankie Santoro might even wear it. I haven't seen any other pop star wearing a golden-retriever-hair jumper. It'd be like cashmere or something. Only I can't spin or knit. If Aunty Helen was here she could teach me. She's so good at making things, like that lovely driftwood statue of you she gave me. But Aunty Helen isn't here – she's teaching in Spain and won't be back till next week – and anyway I haven't got time to learn to knit before Frankie arrives.

So I'll tell you what you missed while you were banished.

I told Gran and Mum about Frankie Santoro over dinner, and Gran was really interested.

'She's that girl who nursed her mother, isn't she?' she said. Gran had brought over one of her homemade shepherd's pies and was serving it out. 'And when she was in the *Songbird* final, her mother was really ill? Lovely girl.'

Gran knows everything there is to know about TV talent shows. Which is funny as Mum won't let me watch them. Mum says they exploit people who don't realise they haven't got any talent. Gran says it's their own fault for going on the shows in the first place, and it's just a bit of fun, and anyway some of them are very talented and have hard lives and it is wonderful to see them succeed after all they have suffered.

Mum used to get really cross about it, but she doesn't get into those arguments any more with Gran. It makes dinner much quieter, but I miss Mum caring so much. All she cares about now is Jack.

I know Mum is right about feeling sorry for people who are rubbish, but it's tricky at school if you never watch any talent shows because everyone keeps talking about them. That's why it's handy having Gran. Sometimes I even manage to be at Gran's when one is on and see it properly. I don't tell Mum, though.

'Yes, that Frankie Santoro is a good girl,' Gran went on, serving a *huge* dollop of shepherd's pie on to my plate.

Mum used to care about that too. She always complained that Gran behaved as if we were being starved. Now she just lets Gran bring over whatever food she wants. Which is usually shepherd's pie. It's nice but you can have a bit too much of it after a while. A bit like Gran. Is that really mean, Timmy?

I'm just fed up with Gran sending you out of the room. It's your home, not hers. Anyway, Gran did a whole speech about Frankie.

'That girl has a beautiful singing voice and she gave up her teenage years to help her mother when she was ill. She deserved to win. I'll never forget the words she said when she won. Do you know what they were?'

Mum and I didn't bother answering as we knew she was going to tell us anyway.

'She said she dedicated her win to her mother, who had done everything for her, and nothing she could do would ever be enough to thank her.'

Gran put a spoonful of shepherd's pie on to her own plate and sat down. I know she would like more than anything in the world for her son to say something like that about her on TV. She'd love Dad to be at a posh award ceremony for amazing journalists. She wouldn't want to be actually there because she doesn't like posh things or fuss, but she'd like her son to be there and say how he couldn't have done it without her.

And it would be true if he said it. Gran didn't get a chance to go to college or anything, even though her teacher said she was very clever and could do anything she liked. She had to bring up Dad and Aunty Helen on her own because their dad died when they were young, and she had to go out to work to clean other people's houses and she didn't get help from anyone.

It's all true, but it's hard to know what to reply when she starts saying it, because she normally talks about no one ever helping her at the same time that she is helping us.

Jack started crying upstairs and Mum got up.

'I'm sure he'll be fine. It's good for him to cry. It will exercise his lungs,' said Gran.

'No. I'll go. Please . . . just stay here . . .' said Mum, and she was off upstairs as if she couldn't get away from us quickly enough.

Your ears are so soft, Timmy.

Where was I? Oh yeah – then Gran started the 'what are you going to do when you grow up?' conversation. You're so lucky nobody asks you anything like that, Timmy.

I don't know why Gran asks me every time she comes over. You'd think she'd be bored.

'So what are you going to be when you grow up, Anna?'

'I don't know, Gran,' I said, for the millionth time. I know she wants me to be a doctor. One day I'm going to tell her I want to be an international jewel thief.

'Well, you'll need to work hard at school whatever you do,' said Gran. 'What's your homework tonight?'

'I've got some geography for tomorrow and I have to write a piece for RS about someone I admire.' Oh no, I suddenly saw Gran look very pleased and hopeful. Hopeful that I might choose her. And I really didn't want to. It would just look weird – everyone is going to write about Frankie Santoro or football players. I love Gran but I don't want to grow up to be like her. Nobody would.

'I think it's got to be someone from history?' I lied. 'I think I'll do Prince Rupert of the Rhine.'

'Prince who of the what?' said Gran, interested. I knew she couldn't mind if I chose someone royal. She has lots of mugs with pictures of the royal family on them.

'Prince Rupert of the Rhine. We learnt about him at primary school. He was a Cavalier in the English Civil War and he had a dog.'

I didn't tell Gran that Prince Rupert got his dog to wee whenever he said the name Oliver Cromwell. I remember telling Mum when we learnt about it in Year 6, and Mum laughed for ages. And don't get any ideas, Timmy. I do NOT want you to learn that trick. Not even if it's when I mention Mrs White. Though that would be funny.

I love it when you roll over like that, you big soppy dog.

You've never been very good at tricks. Not normal ones, anyway. Or even bringing balls back. In fact, you are *rubbish* at retrieving. You are a golden 'please will you retrieve the ball for me while I wag my tail' dog.

But you are good at wiggling your eyebrows. First one, then the other.

That's a talent too.

Gran has finished hoovering. I'll do a bit of violin practice. Miss Green says I have made a very good start and that everyone has problems with tuning at the beginning. The important thing is to practice.

That's not fair. Gran made LOADS of noise hoovering. I don't see why she thinks Jack will wake up and get upset if I play the violin.

Good. Gran's gone.

I'll go online and look up Prince Rupert. I'm not sure I should say the bit about his dog and I don't have many other things to say. I don't want Tanesha and Caitlin and Suzi rolling their eyes and saying I'm so immature.

Though it is funny.

Mum's been looking up a lot of clinics. Why's she doing that?

I suppose I shouldn't have looked at her search

history. Or clicked on the links. But it's really awful. There are all these babies born early like Jack, and they can't walk, and they have to be treated at special clinics in America. Is that what is going to happen to Jack? I don't want to think about it. Mum's probably just checking things. Jack's too small to walk, anyway.

I'll look up Prince Rupert. His dog was called Boye, and Boye cocked his leg when he heard the name John Pym, not Oliver Cromwell. He was a white hunting poodle, not a retriever like you, Timmy.

Timmy? Hey – what have you got? Where did you find that? I thought I heard a clatter. You've got to stop raiding the bin. It's no good just wagging your tail like that. Oh, it's okay, soppy dog. You don't have to lick me to death.

Good night, Timberoni macaroni, pasta-eating superhero, anything-eating superhero. Good night, Tim the bin.

Tuesday

Chapter Four

You really like dental sticks, don't you? Basically, you're brushing your teeth AND eating the toothbrush afterwards. Actually, I don't want to think about that too much.

Sorry it was such a rush this morning. We all overslept. Mum and Jack were up most of the night. I forgot to set my alarm and I didn't wake up until eight and then I had to run for the bus. I was quite pleased I was so fast.

Mrs Berlinski took the register and then turned into Mad Music Teacher. She is *really* excited about Frankie Santoro coming.

Right, 7B!' she announced. 'We want *all* of Year 7 to be involved with Frankie Santoro's visit. So, from now until she arrives we're going to spend music lessons and form periods working on the bands.'

That showed Suzi Lyons. I could see her and

Tanesha and Caitlin really scowling. So much for them being the only Year 7 band.

Mrs Berlinski said that we would be making the bands in groups of four. She gave Caitlin, Suzi and Tanesha Brendan O'Donoghue because he sits near them. They looked really pleased, because according to them he is the best-looking boy in the class, but he looked really fed up. I think he wanted to be with Alex Black and Wesley Douglas and Oliver Sheppard. Alex was at St Faith's with us, Brendan came from Ireland and Wesley and Oliver were at Bekesbourne Primary, but they're always together now. They play football every break. That's all they ever talk about. If Suzi and the others don't choose a football song I bet Brendan won't sing.

We were lucky we were sitting together already – but guess who we are stuck with just because she sits next to Emma? Lauren. AND we have been given M1 practice room, which Emma says smells of wet socks. Wesley Douglas said it's haunted and the smell of wet socks only shows there has been poltergeist activity. He watches a lot of TV programmes about ghosts. Emma says it's because Wesley dries his football kit on the radiator in there (Mrs Berlinski would go mad if she found out) but Wesley says that has nothing to do with it and his socks don't smell. I wouldn't know because I can't smell very well anyway. That reminds me of one of Mum's jokes:

My dog's got no nose.

How does he smell?

Terrible.

I suppose it's quite a useful gift. I could be a secret agent and be sent into smelly areas where others could not go.

'It's not fair Lauren is in our group,' muttered Emma as we carried our chairs out to M1. 'She's going to spoil everything.'

'What can you do?' she asked Lauren, straight out, when we had got our chairs in a circle. It was the first time any of us had spoken to Lauren for ages.

'I can sing,' said Lauren.

'That's no good,' said Emma. 'Mohona is the singer in the band.'

'I don't mind, honestly,' said Mohona. 'Let Lauren do it.'

'No. We have to rely on the singer, and Lauren's hardly ever here,' said Emma. 'I'm playing guitar and Anna is playing violin. You'll just have to play the tambourine or something, Lauren. That way if you don't turn up it won't ruin everything.'

That seems a bit mean, but Emma knows what she is talking about. Lauren was Emma's partner for lasagne back in September, and she turned up without the minced meat so Emma, who had brought in all the pasta and milk and cheese, had to borrow some frozen vegetables from the food tech freezer and Mrs White helped her make a vegetable lasagne instead, and Emma said her dad was really disappointed when she brought it home. And Lauren didn't even say sorry when she came into school the next day. So I can see why Emma didn't trust her. At least I said sorry about the fish.

Lauren didn't argue with Emma, but she looked a bit fed up. Mrs Berlinski said we could use Emma's phone to look up songs, so we looked up 'Loving You' by Dylan Williams because I remembered he sang it as a guest on *X-Factor*. Gran's a big fan. I think his grandad was in a home or something and when Dylan got rich he took him on holiday. Gran read about it in the hairdresser's. She likes stories like that. She doesn't like him quite as much as Frankie because looking after your mum is a bit better than taking your grandad on holiday, but he's definitely up there.

We found the guitar chords for Emma online and I got my violin to work out the tune. It's quite difficult, actually. Lauren didn't join in. She just sat on the chair leafing through music, ignoring us. She couldn't even be bothered to look for a tambourine. Mohona kept singing very quietly and looking over at her, worried she wasn't joining in, but Emma just said, 'Leave her, Mohona. She won't turn up anyway,' and Lauren went on blanking us so we just carried on until the bell went.

'I think we need a bit of practice,' said Emma as we packed up. 'We'll meet up at lunchtime tomorrow. Let's see if M2 is free. I can't stand Wesley's socks any more.'

I got a merit in geography. I was a bit worried as I forgot to do my homework about ways to save the planet, but I remembered Mum's shop and I said one way we could care for the earth was to not buy so many new clothes, but wear vintage clothes, which would be better for the environment, and Mr Cassidy said, 'Excellent, Anna,' which was pretty amazing as normally he just says things like, 'I can't believe you've forgotten your work again' or something about my writing being too messy. It's the first time really he's ever been nice to me. Of course Suzi Lyons tried to spoil it and muttered loudly, 'Who wants to wear old clothes?' but Emma said, 'Frankie Santoro for one' and it was brilliant. Suzi Lyons just glared at us.

We had double French then. It was fun. I told Madame Saulnier I had '*un chien et un petit frère*'. I also learnt that 'I have a golden retriever' is '*J'ai un golden retriever*'. So it's easy to talk about you in two languages, Tim!

The next thing the bell was ringing and we were charging downstairs to lunch and choir practice. Mrs Berlinski has chosen 'He Ain't Heavy, He's My Brother' as the song we will sing to Frankie, which is a bit odd, I think. She says it's because Frankie is founding a charity about helping people, but it's a bit slow and gloomy, not like Frankie's songs. I really like them because you can dance to them. I'll play you some later, Timmy.

I've just had a fantastic idea! If you were in our band we could get you to dance with us at the audition, Timmy. I wish I'd trained you by now. When we got you they said your mum and dad were in a golden retriever dance display team. Mum and I were going to find out if there were classes near us. But then Jack came along and stuff so we didn't get round to it.

Anyway, maybe we don't need classes. Maybe you're just naturally talented. Maybe there will be something on YouTube about dog dancing and I can teach you in secret and then bring you to school for the video and you'll be brilliant and they will choose us for Frankie's video. That would be AMAZING.

I suppose I'd better take you out for a walk. Mum's upstairs with Jack so that should cheer her up. She worries we don't take you out enough.

You were AWFUL, Timmy. How am I going to teach you to dance if you won't even walk to heel? You used to be so much better at puppy class. It was only a squirrel. You nearly pulled my arm off. And then how would I play violin for the audition?

I'll go and check on Mum and Jack. Have a dog biscuit. Though you don't really deserve it.

Mum says she doesn't want any dinner. I'll just do some pasta, then. Luckily I found a jar of pesto in the cupboard.

I'm feeling quite good about cooking suddenly.

We are making pizza in food tech tomorrow. I'm completely sorted. Dad and I went into town on Saturday before he went away and I bought the cheese myself. I wrapped it up and I wrote 'Anna's cheese for Wednesday' on it and put it in the fridge. I bought a packet of herbs too. I should have bought some bicarbonate of soda, but I didn't know what aisle it was in. I didn't want to ask in case they knew it was for greasy hair. Anyway, Mohona is bringing the flour and the margarine and the yeast and the tomatoes. I feel really sorry for Emma having Lauren as a partner again, but she says she's just going to bring in everything, just in case.

Wednesday

Chapter Five

Sorry for waking you, Tim. I know you were asleep in your basket (well, it is two o'clock) and I know you can't do anything, but it helps just to tell you.

Okay, you've fallen asleep again. I'll just sit here and look at you, then. I love the way you're lying at my feet and twitching your paws and wagging your tail in your sleep. It's thumping on the floor and I think that means you must be having lovely dreams. I wish I was in those dreams with you.

I keep thinking about Mum and Dad. Fancy arguing about nappies on Skype. That's not what it was invented for.

I thought it was going to be a good night. Mum got out of bed after all and she got dressed and came downstairs and it was lovely at first. She said she was sorry she had been half asleep when I had come to see her and that she'd changed her mind about dinner and how pleased she was about the merit mark from geography. Then she went into the kitchen and put music on and cooked a special dinner just for me and her. Then we went to Skype Dad.

It was fine at first. We said 'hello' as usual and Dad asked Mum what we were up to, and Mum said Jack was asleep and she had made a lovely cheesy bake for me and her, and Dad said, 'Yum' and that he wished he was with us, and then he asked Mum what she was going to do later, and Mum said she was going to sort out the nappy buckets, and Dad said, 'Why don't you give yourself a break, Liz, and get disposable nappies?' He was only trying to be nice. To be honest, he's quietly been getting as fed up as me with all the buckets of cloth nappies in the kitchen every time he comes home, and I was really glad he said something about it. Even I can smell them. Mum won't let Dad do anything about them when he is here, but she never seems to finish sorting them out. They are always either soaking in buckets waiting to be washed or being washed or hanging out to dry or on Jack being made dirty all over again. And in the meantime all our other washing is piling up in an endless queue for the washing machine.

Anyway, Mum went mad. She went from all relaxed and talking about dinner to absolutely furious. She didn't even ask me to leave the room – she just sort of exploded.

'I'm not making things difficult, Simon. And I am not going to fill up landfills with rubbish to make you feel better. What do you care, anyway? You're away for two whole weeks this time.'

'That's not fair, Liz,' said Dad. 'I'll be back before you know it.' Even on the screen I could see he looked upset, and the delay in his words made them sound sadder. I suppose I should have left the room but I really wanted to tell Dad about my day. I wished Mum hadn't talked about nappies. Then Jack started screaming. Mum ran upstairs to him. She looked glad to leave us. She was so angry, Timmy. Angrier than just an argument about nappies could make anyone.

She's never been like that before. She's only started shouting since Jack came. I just remember taking it for granted that Mum and Dad never argued. I thought they were the perfect match. Dad is quiet but kind. Mum is more – not exactly loud – just busy. She's always got ideas and she used to be so happy, getting in the clothes for the shop, or acting in her drama group.

'Anna, can you bring up some wipes?' she called down.

'Um – I just want to talk to Dad,' I called, hanging about in front of the screen. I could see Dad running his fingers through his hair the way he does when he is worried.

'Never mind, Anna. Go and help your mum,' he said sadly. 'I won't be able to Skype for a day or two as I'm doing an interview in a remote mountain village, but I'll be in touch soon. I love you,' and he ended the session.

He ended the session, Tim. I didn't even get to tell him about my merit mark. I stood there, alone in the kitchen, hearing Jack crying and crying upstairs.

'Anna, would you hurry up and bring me those wipes?' yelled Mum, really crossly. She never used to yell like that.

Last night wasn't a good night after all, Timmy.

Thanks for the lick. I think I'll try to go back to bed now.

I'm so tired. We didn't sleep that well last night, did we Timmy? But at least I've packed my planner and I've made myself a tuna sandwich. I'm getting really good at sandwiches. I just need to get the cheese for food tech out of the fridge and I'm ready.

My cheese has gone. Mum must have used it all for the cheesy bake last night. I've got no cheese.

I've got no cheese, Timmy.

The others will have left by now. It's too late to ask them and I haven't got time to go to the shops. I can't believe it, Timmy. That was all I was supposed to bring. And I haven't got it. I've got to turn up and say:

'Thanks, Mohona for bringing the flour and the margarine, the tomatoes and the herbs. Sorry about the cheese. It's not as if it's important. In a cheese and tomato pizza. Don't you agree, Mrs White?'

You won't need your supersonic canine hearing to hear her answer:

NO!

Chapter Six

Hey – calm down, Tim – I can't let you out in the garden if you keep jumping in front of the door.

That was fast.

Maybe we should have called you Dash.

Did I tell you we had a whole list of names for you? On the way to pick you up from Mrs Delaney we argued about what we were going to call you. You were the last one left. Mum teased me and said, 'Gnasher', Dad said, 'Goldie' for golden retriever, but I wasn't sure. Aunty Helen said, 'Shadow'. Emma thought Snoopy or Gromit but I knew you wouldn't look like those names. Then Mrs Delaney said she hoped we didn't mind, but she'd named you already because you were the runt of the litter and she didn't know if you'd survive. She said she'd called you it because it was snowing when you were born and she'd thought of Tiny Tim from *A Christmas Carol*.

We could have changed it if we'd wanted to, but as soon as Mum and Dad told me about who Tiny Tim was and I saw you, so small and adorable, I knew it was your name.

Though you're not so tiny now, are you?

You're like that dog in the story who gets bigger with love. Clifford the Big Red Dog.

Timford.

You must feel better now that you've done a wee. Maybe I should take you out for a quick walk. It looks like Mum is asleep.

Well, that was a bit of a disaster. Just because that lady at the bus stop patted you and said you were very beautiful on our way up the street, didn't mean you had to practically pull me across the road to see her again when we were coming back down.

You were awful. Maybe Mum hasn't managed to walk you much.

I'm going to make a list of things I have to teach you NOT to want to chase:

1. Cats
2. Leaves
3. Empty crisp packets
4. Squirrels

You're just like Doug in *Up*. We'll have to watch that together. It would be so cool if we could get you a collar so I could hear you speak like him.

Come and have a biscuit. We can see if there's anything good on TV, and I'll tell you what happened today.

I wasn't the only person who didn't have cheese in food tech, and luckily Mrs White found out about Lauren before me. She really screamed at her.

'Change your attitude, young woman, or you'll get nowhere in life.' Lauren just stared ahead and didn't look at her, and that made Mrs White even more angry.

'Right. Lunchtime detention today, and this morning you can sort out the cupboards. There is no point in you cooking pizza without cheese.'

'Can't I make bread?' said Lauren. I couldn't believe it. Nobody talks back to Mrs White.

Mrs White was speechless for a moment. 'No. We

are making pizza, and you are coming with me to sort out the cupboards.'

I felt sick. 'Mohona – I've forgotten my cheese too,' I whispered as Mrs White frogmarched Lauren to the corner with the cupboards and gave her a pen and paper to write down what was in them.

'I want it all neat and tidy and itemised by the end of the lesson. And if you finish early you can give the shelves a wipe. I'll be back to check,' said Mrs White loudly. She was in such a bad mood.

'It's okay, Anna. Mum gave me some just in case,' Mohona said quietly. She smiled at me, but I felt a bit weird. It's like Mohona's mum expected me to forget. Mostly, though, I felt relieved. Especially when Mrs White stomped over to our table. Mohona had already laid out the utensils very neatly, and Mrs White couldn't find anything to be angry about.

'Thanks, Mohona. You saved my life,' I whispered. That was LITERALLY true, Timmy. Mrs White is the meanest teacher in the world.

Mrs White made a big thing of getting cheese out of the fridge and giving it to Emma. 'You didn't let your partner down, and it isn't fair you should suffer because of her,' she said.

'Sorry, Mohona,' I whispered.

'It's okay,' she said.

Mohona put her hair back in a ponytail. She lent me an elastic band too so I could do the same. Mohona always looks so tidy. Even though she wears exactly the same uniform as everyone else, it just looks different somehow. Better. Not like mine. I don't know why, but no matter how I put on my skirt, the zip on the side always slips around to the front, and my blouse comes untucked. My tights always have ladders, but I'm going to start freezing them. I'm hoping I can stop looking a mess and be more like Emma and Mohona. Mrs White calls me a walking disaster. She thinks that's funny. She always seems to see me when I am rushing from one class to another, and I always end up dropping something when I pass her.

But today the pizza was a TRIUMPH! I think even Mrs White was secretly impressed. We did NOTHING wrong and she had to give us each an A. An A from Mrs White, Timmy. Unheard of.

I did forget to put on my apron at first, and I did manage to drop a big dollop of sauce on my jumper, but Mohona quickly passed me an apron and I put it on before Mrs White turned round and caught me. I'd better write that down:

1. Sort out jumper.

I keep forgetting things. We had an assembly about it where they told us forgetting things was normal. That it was part of growing up and perfectly natural and to do with chemicals in the brain. But they still give you detention when you forget your homework. Anyway, they said to use memory aids, like Post-its or reminders on your phone, or lists. I like writing lists. I can write them on the back of envelopes, like Gran does, so I'm not even wasting paper. There's always loads of envelopes from Jack's hospital appointments.

As soon as food tech was over Emma found us.
'I can't believe Lauren!' she said. 'She's so selfish. Now we have to have our first band practice without her because she's in detention. And she doesn't care about the band, anyway. It's not fair we're stuck with her.'
At least we had two nice teachers after horrible Mrs White. We're reading *Oliver Twist* in English

with Miss Lacey, and then maths was fun because Mr Hawkins made us use dominoes to revise prime numbers. Then we met up at lunchtime in the music room. We brought our sandwiches with us, which technically we weren't supposed to do, but it was an emergency. We don't have much time before Frankie comes.

The first thing we have to do is find a name. 'If we don't have a good name they won't notice us,' said Emma, opening her crisp packet.

'Shouldn't we be practising the song?' said Mohona.

'Yes, but we have to have a name first,' said Emma.

'How about going through the alphabet? So A – what name could work beginning with A?' I said.

'Hey! A-mazing. And that also works because we all have an A at the end of our names,' said Mohona. Emm-A, Ann-A, Mohon-A'. She picked up a marker that was by the white board and wrote it up.

A-Mazing

'But Lauren doesn't end with an A,' said Emma.
'There's an A in it,' I said. 'It's just not at the end.'

'No, it's no good,' said Emma, crossing it out. If we didn't have Lauren it would really work. But her name ruins it.'

We sat for a bit staring at the blank board. I ate my sandwich. Mohona crunched her apple. Emma finished her crisps and scrumpled up the packet.

'I know!' said Emma, throwing it in the bin and brushing the crisp crumbs off her hands. 'We can use a random name generator. I'll find one on my phone.'

It came up with some really strange names: Gary Turnip, Simply and the Guys, Wednesday Alliance, Monday Busters, Floppy Cranberry, Meteor Quotations. I quite liked that one, but Emma didn't.

'We can put a word in to help with the band name,' said Emma.

'How about "romantic"?' said Mohona. 'We're singing Dylan Williams's song and he is really romantic.' Mohona really likes Dylan Williams.

That was even worse. We put 'romantic' into the name generator and we got names like Romantic Skeleton, Romantic Carrot, Yellow Romantic and Afterglow Romantic of the Aqua Feet.

'I'm going to look up another band-name website,' Emma said. 'Look – this one isn't random

– it says we just have to find five words that make us think about the music we're singing and make a name out of them. So we've got to think about Dylan Williams's song.'

'So, like handsome?' said Mohona, finishing her apple and starting on her roll.

'No – Dylan Williams is handsome, not the song,' said Emma.

'Let's try romantic again,' said Mohona. She's a bit obsessed.

'It says we can have our names in it too,' said Emma.

'But that's four of the words already,' said Mohona. 'Romantic Emma, Anna, Mohona, Lauren.' She wrote them on the board and we looked at it. 'That's not a very good band name,' Mohona said.

'The initials spell REAML – REALM – that could be our name,' I said. 'I know! Romantic Realm! That's got romantic in it, Mohona, and it's also sort of us like ruling the world – like we are the best.'

'No. I don't want us to say we are romantic in our band name,' said Emma, shaking her head. 'Imagine what the boys would say.'

There was a moment's silence whilst we thought of the horror of it. Mohona gave a disappointed sigh.

Emma was right.

'Let's write some adjectives anyway,' I said. 'Why do we like Dylan Williams? Why are we singing his music? Apart from fancying him, Mohona.'

'It's sort of loud and upbeat,' said Emma.

'It makes you feel happy. It's . . . chirpy and poppy,' said Mohona. She wrote more names on the board.

Loud Realm

Upbeat Realm.

Chirpy Realm.

Poppy Realm

'We could wear poppies?' said Mohona in desperation. 'We could all wear red and put poppies all over your guitar, Emma?'

'We're not singing about the First World War, Mohona,' said Emma.

'We should wear something "different", though,' I said. 'What about some clothes from Mum's shop?' I said. 'Vintage clothes are unique. Frankie Santoro loves them.'

'Brilliant!" said Emma.

I looked in my bag for my orange, and I saw my maths book.

'Dominoes!' I said. 'We can call our band The

Dominoes and we can wear black and white vintage clothes and hats and gloves and stuff '

'That's a BRILLIANT idea!' said Emma. 'And black and white is like black and white films, and that's really romantic, Mohona.'

The bell rang for the end of lunch. We hadn't actually practised our music but we had a name and our costumes were going to be awesome.

We heard Wesley Douglas and James Peters and Alex Black and Oliver Sheppard walking down the corridor. James was looking at his phone.

'Okay – so we're Steve Turnip and the Spiders,' I heard him say.

'That's cool!' said Wesley.

But it really isn't.

Chapter Seven

Right. I've coloured in the diagram for chemistry and packed it in my bag ready to give in tomorrow.

I think that's the only way I'm going to keep on top of things at secondary school. Just do homework as soon as I am given it. I feel pretty good about it, Timmy. This is the new me. I'm going to finish my list:

1. Sort out jumper.
2. Get ingredients for fruit salad next week.
3. Practise violin.

I am determined not to let Mohona down again. And violin's much harder than I thought it would be. Oh, and –

4. Sort out when we should go to Mum's shop to borrow some vintage clothes.

Mum's not working there at the moment because of all the stuff with Jack, but Matt is running it for her.

So now I'm going to be super-organised and start at number one. My jumper. I am SO glad Mrs White didn't see. It's all covered in dog hair as well.

I suppose that's your fault, Timmy. But I forgive you. And I can do something about the dog hair as long as I have some Sellotape. It picks it up really well. That was something Mum told me. But the jumper does need a wash. I've been wearing it for ages.

I can't believe it's seven o'clock already. Mum just came down and put some nappies in the wash and some in the bucket and then went back to bed with Jack. He never seems to be in his cot.

I took Mum half of my pizza from school on a tray. She said it was lovely. And Jack looked very sweet asleep. I hope he'll stop crying so much and I can get to cuddle him a bit more. Mum said she needed to go to sleep for a bit, as she is very, very tired. If Jack stopped crying I might see her more too.

I wish I could Skype Dad tonight, but he's off doing that interview in the mountains. I know it's really good he got that job, but I do miss him, Timmy.

You're so lovely to hug. I'm so glad I've got you.

It was good you were named Tim. I know it was for Tiny Tim, but I used to pretend I was George from *The Famous Five* and you were her dog, Timmy. Do you remember when you were a puppy and I made a tent out of some blankets and a wooden stick, and tried to make you camp with me at the bottom of the garden, but you got so excited you grabbed the tent pole to chew and knocked it over? Then I tried to teach you to sleep at the bottom of my bed like Timmy did on George's bed, but you chewed a pillow and Mum and Dad said you had to sleep downstairs. It's just as well Mum and Dad said no. You're much too big to share a bed now.

I'm not sure how good you'd be at tracking down smugglers like Timmy in the book, either. The postman says you're the friendliest dog on his rounds. You think everyone is lovely. Perhaps we should concentrate on your dancing instead. Wait a minute. I'll find it on YouTube. Come and have a look.

That's your mum and dad, Timmy. Dancing at Crufts. The Golden Retriever Dance Display Team.

You're like Posy in *Ballet Shoes*. It's in your blood. You were born to dance. That's probably why you're so rubbish at retrieving and spotting enemies and stuff like that. It doesn't matter, we'll just concentrate on dancing and we'll start now. We just need to look up how to do it. I'll put on Dylan Williams and we can work out a routine.

Okay, Timmy. Ready? I've got the treats. So, 1) We're going to get you to go round in a circle. That'll be at the beginning of the song, and then 2) I'm going to do the move where I walk and you go through my legs.

I've got a really good feeling about this. Nobody else will have a dancing dog. I think Frankie Santoro will love it. She might even ask us to support her on a tour.

SIT.

Right. Let me put the music on.

No. STAY.

Okay. Let's start.

Circle. No. Stop. SIT. Okay. Circle. NO.

Maybe there's not enough room. Let's just try walking.

Oh, Timmy. That was HOPELESS. Don't look so sad. It was only our first go. It's not your fault. You haven't had any practice. You did your best. Have a treat anyway.

Thursday

Chapter Eight

Oh no, Timmy! How did you get so muddy? I only let you out in the garden for a bit. I'm going to let Mum and Jack sleep as they had a bad night. I'd better keep you in your area, as Mum will get really upset if she wakes up and finds you've got mud in the house.

So, I've done my sandwiches. Today I am experimenting a bit. I have tried Marmite and cheese as my Thursday combination. If it is a big success then perhaps we could also make sandwiches and give them to the TV crew, and they might ask us to present a food tech TV show for children. It's good to have a back-up plan as well as the band.

I'm going to start a list of sandwiches:

1. Marmite and cheese
2. Jam
3. Marmalade

4. Egg — but only free range.
5. Cucumber

(Gran likes those because she thinks the queen has them at garden parties.)

6. Peanut butter
7. Ham

But only ham from outdoor reared pigs because Mum always says that if the animal wasn't looked after properly we shouldn't eat the meat. But lots of people don't eat meat at all. So maybe it will be easier if we just do vegetarian sandwiches.

I'll ask Emma and Mohona if they have any other ideas for combinations. Emma's parents have a café in town and Emma's brother Ramon makes amazing sandwiches there on Saturdays. He is going out with Priya Bennet, the head girl, and he looks like he could be a pop star. Emma says he writes songs so maybe he will be famous one day. Maybe he'll even write one for Frankie Santoro.

The kitchen looks a bit of a mess. I think I'll try to load the dishwasher before school. I don't want to go near the nappies.

The post has come already and I can see Mum's friend Sandra has sent something. This is a) good because Mum loves getting post from Sandra and b) bad because Dad doesn't really like what Sandra's post makes Mum do.

Sandra is Mum's best friend from school and she lives miles away, but Dad says it feels like she is always with us. I don't think he means that as a compliment. She sort of gets involved with everything. Like when Mum was pregnant. Sandra sent all these books and vitamin supplements and meditation music. It was a bit funny coming home and finding Mum asleep with her huge tummy, while whale music filled the sitting room.

You didn't seem to mind, Tim – it used to send you to sleep too. Whale music is really eerie and beautiful. I'm not sure what the whales are singing about, but you feel like you're floating when you hear it. And Sandra sent a dreamcatcher for Mum, and Mum hung it over their bed, and then laughed when Dad kept bumping into it. She said it must be because he was her dream man but she let him hang it in the window then. I thought it was beautiful with all its feathers and beads, so I went into town and got one from Fiesta and Mohona and Emma both got one as well. I love my dreamcatcher.

Aunty Helen likes dreamcatchers too. She's got lots of them in her cottage. Do you remember when you jumped up and ate one? She didn't mind, though. She said you'd probably seen a really bad dream stuck in it and wanted to get rid of it for her. Then you were sick, which she said proved her point. She said a good dream wouldn't have made you sick. She says good things have good results.

I love Aunty Helen. It's so cool having an artist as an aunt. I think I'd like to be an artist. Or a pop star. Or a dog trainer. A dog whisperer, I think they call it. Though I don't really whisper to you. I think I'd be a dog chatterer.

Anyway, Timmy, I'd better go. Here's some clean water to keep you going until Mum comes down. Sorry I couldn't take you for a walk. The nappy buckets smell so much, I think I'll put them outside the garden door. I'll leave a note to tell Mum where they are. And now I've got a paw print on my skirt.

Chapter Nine

Shh. I don't want Gran to know you're in my room.
I just need a cuddle after school.

Get out of my bag, Timmy. There's nothing to
eat. Just lie down and let me talk to you.

I know I've already had one cuddle this evening.
It was nice holding Jack. Strange, but nice. I suppose
I haven't really done it much. First he had all those
tubes, and since they got back from hospital he's
always been asleep, or crying upstairs with Mum.

When I got back from school Gran was here. She
had cleaned the kitchen, and made a cake. It looked
fantastic. Mum was sitting in the armchair and she
was dressed, and Gran put Jack in my arms and went
off to start dinner.

Jack's really sweet, isn't he? He's the only baby
I've ever held, and he's so small. Too small, the health
visitor says. Like they said he would be. But his little

fingernails are so cute. I love how he's got tiny ears and eyelashes and his eyes, when they are open, are sort of gentle and new. I do love him. It's just that sooner or later he starts arching his back or being sick and then Mum wants to take him again, so it's hard to relax.

Jack opened his eyes and I was worried he would start crying, but he didn't. He just fell asleep again.

'How was your day, Anna?' Mum said. It felt like ages since she'd asked that. I wanted to run over and give her a big hug, but I didn't want to wake Jack. And then he started crying, so Mum took him back and I said I had some homework to do and went upstairs with a slice of Gran's cake. And you, Timmy.

Because, after all, I did want to tell someone about my day.

So, first of all, I nearly missed the bus but I did this amazing sprint and jumped on just before it drove off, but then I sort of staggered down the aisle. I leaned against the luggage thingy, panting a bit and hoping I wouldn't need my inhaler, and then the bus went round the corner and I fell in. Right in. My legs were sort of hooked over the side and I kept waving my arms but I couldn't get up, and I was holding my skirt so it didn't fall down, which made it even more difficult to do anything.

And it seemed like for ages nobody was admitting they had seen me. I heard some Year 9 boys laughing at the other end of the bus, but I couldn't see if it was at me. I was sort of hoping they were laughing at someone else, like Stinky Brown in Year 8.

Anyway, then Priya Bennet, the head girl, the one who is going out with Emma's brother, came to my rescue. She's so nice. She pulled me out and asked me if I was okay, and I said I was, and then I spent the rest of the journey bright red, facing the front, not meeting anyone's eyes and hoping that any laughter I heard was nothing to do with me. Perhaps people were just telling a lot of jokes this morning.

It was good, though, because I told Mohona and Emma about it and they really laughed, and that made it feel completely different. Mohona laughed so much that she cried. She's great to tell stories to.

Then we had textiles, where I broke a needle in the sewing machine, and French, where we had a test that I had completely forgotten about so I didn't exactly do well. In one way I did. You could almost say I got one hundred per cent, because I got the words right if you said them the way that I spelled them. I was right about the words, just not the accents or the order of the letters. I said that to Mohona at lunch (by the way, you can have half a cheese and Marmite sandwich if you like – it turns out that I don't like it) and she thought it was really funny too. I love making people laugh.

Right, that cake was delicious. I'm going to go down and have dinner now. I've got to make sure I eat everything Gran gives me or she'll say I had too much cake. Though I don't actually think that's possible.

I think I might ask Gran if I can put my uniform in when the washing machine is empty. I've got my jumper hanging out the window to get a bit of air.

Sorry you're back in your area again, Timmy. Gran wasn't very impressed when she caught me taking you downstairs. I don't know why your paws thunder so much. You wouldn't be very good as a secret-agent dog.

At least you've got a bone. And you don't have homework or anything to do.

Gran was telling me again at dinner about how hard Dad and Aunty Helen worked at their homework when they were my age, and then Mum suddenly started telling us about her letter from Sandra.

'Sandra's sent me an information pack about a doctor in America called Dr King and he has discovered that if you give special exercises to premature babies then they don't have any problems with their muscles later.'

'That's good,' I said.

'It's absolutely wonderful. Sandra thinks we can start a fundraising campaign and advertise it on Facebook.'

'Why do we need a fundraising campaign?' I said.

'Because you can only get his special treatment if you go to his clinic in America. I want to take Jack there to make sure he doesn't develop any muscle problems.'

'What does Simon think about it?' said Gran. You could see she wasn't very keen on the idea but was trying very hard not to argue with Mum.

'Simon? Oh, he doesn't know about it. I've only just got the letter from Sandra and of course I can't contact him yet. But he'll be so excited, I know he will,' said Mum. 'I'm sorry – I've need to start researching it now. This is a lovely meal, but I've got to make the most of the time now Jack is asleep. I'm going to Skype Sandra.'

Then she got up and left the table, leaving half her dinner.

'Well!' said Gran, looking very cross and offended.

It was a bit rude of Mum. But it's important because it's going to help Jack get better. I'll tell Mohona and Emma and maybe we can get involved in the fundraising.

Anyway, because Mum was on the computer, I couldn't use it to do my homework so I cleared the table and loaded the dishwasher. The washing was still going around so I took out my violin and tried to practise, but Gran asked me to stop again in case it woke up Jack. So I thought I would start my own joke book and wrote down some jokes I know. But I'm not all that good at remembering the punchlines, and basically they are the best bit. It's no good saying something like someone goes to a zoo and sees a lion talking to a crocodile if you can't actually remember what they said.

Still, I have managed to start a play. I'm writing it in the notebook Emma gave me for my birthday, and with the pen I got from Mohona. It's a bit like *High School Musical* and a bit like *Downton Abbey* and a bit like one of the old musicals with Fred Astaire that Mum and I used to curl up together and watch on Sunday afternoons. Maybe that's something we can be doing when the TV team are touring the school. They can see us acting and maybe interview us.

So far it's:

Girl in long brown coat and hat from Mum's shop (Elizabeth): Hello, I love your dress, Sylvia.

Girl in flowery dress (Sylvia): Hello, Elizabeth, your hat is beautiful.

Girl in another flowery dress (Charlotte): Is anyone going to the ball tomorrow?

Elizabeth: Yes, but I can't dance.

Charlotte: Anyone can dance, Elizabeth!

And then there'll be a song or something, and Sylvia and Charlotte will dance. Maybe with brooms. I'm not sure where they are. Maybe a park, and there are those brooms to sweep up leaves and they can dance about. Maybe they can even tap dance and

Elizabeth can watch them.

I know! There could be a dog. There could be a dog in the park – like you – and it could join in and do an amazing dance with Elizabeth. Who ends up being a brilliant dancer. And then she can sing something.

<u>Anyone can dance!</u>

Anyone can dance! Anyone at all!
Even a golden retriever can go to a ball!

Or *Even a retriever can go to a ball.* Yes, that fits better. Then something about birds. Like anyone can sing, wings, things. I know!

Just like it's not only birds who can sing
If you just believe you can do anything.

Something about 'chance' and 'dance'.

So now I've decided to take this new chance,
Something something something, dance dance dance!

I'd definitely go and see it if it was a film.

Of course we couldn't actually bring you to school for the rehearsal, but we could tell the TV people about you.

We could even show them a photo of you in a hat.

Do you remember when we put a cloche hat and a feather boa on you, and Mum laughed so much, and we took a photograph of you and put it up in the shop and someone bought the hat and the boa because of it. The photo is still up by the till.

Don't worry, though. You wouldn't have to wear a hat in the play. Dad said that boys had to stick together and he was not going to let us dress you up any more.

I think Dad is pretty glad Jack has come. That's one more boy in the family – you, Dad and Jack. Actually, it's three–two now. Mum and I are outnumbered.

Unless we count Gran. But I'd rather not. She can stay in the extended family bit. Even if she only lives around the corner. I'm so glad she doesn't actually live WITH us.

Even if her cake is completely yummy.

Chapter Ten

Mum sounded really happy Skyping Sandra. I even heard her laugh a bit. So I didn't want to say, 'Um, excuse me, I really need the computer to do my homework.' Actually, that's exactly what I wanted to say, but I couldn't, because it was nice hearing Mum laughing and sounding excited.

So I went upstairs to look for my homework planner, and then Gran called me down.

'Anna, could you come downstairs? I'd like a nice chat with you.'

Though it's not exactly what I'd call it.

Gran's idea of a nice chat was to say that the buckets of nappies smelt and we couldn't just put them out in the garden and ignore them. If Mum wouldn't agree to buy disposable ones, she said, then I'd just have to help out a bit more as she didn't have the time and she'd done enough in her own day with two children and no hard-working husband to support her and no money to buy disposable nappies even if there were any, thank you very much. I think she was still cross about Mum leaving the dinner.

'You're a big girl now, Anna. I can help from time to time, but I have my own life. I'm going away to visit my friend Edie for a few days and I don't want to leave you and your mother in this state. I'm going to teach you how to wash these nappies so that this house doesn't smell to high heaven when your poor father comes home, and so your brother has something to wear.'

'NO! UGH! AAAGH!' is what I thought. 'Okay,' is what I said. Because Gran was right. Mum isn't coping with the nappies. So I didn't want to help and I did, if you know what I mean. Like when we're on a walk, Timmy, and you really want to run away after a rabbit, but we call you and then you come running back for a treat instead because you want that more. The thing I want more is for everything to go back to normal, Mum to be happier and Jack to be well.

'The ones in the washing machine have been washed, but they haven't been taken out,' Gran said.

'So they've got smelly and need to be washed again at a very high temperature. Look.' She put the washing powder in the compartment and turned the knob to the hottest temperature and the whole thing started up again before I could put my uniform in.

It was like someone jumping the queue at the bus stop. I hate that. Especially when they do it and then it's your turn to get on and the driver says, 'Sorry, full up, you'll have to wait for the next one.' The worst ones for that are Kirsty Stewart and her friends from Year 9. And coming home it's those two old ladies who always complain very loudly about schoolchildren and then suddenly rush forward and push on before us. I bet they were the Kirsty Stewarts of their day.

Anyway, I'd missed my chance. The suds were gathering in the window of the machine, the water was swishing, and the nappies were going round and round. Again. Luckily my uniform doesn't look too bad. It'll do again for tomorrow.

'So, these dirty ones in the bucket need to be sluiced in the toilet. You're a lucky girl to have two toilets, Anna. And your washing machine is so much better than the twin tub I had to use. Really, you young ones don't know you're born sometimes.'

I wanted to say 'Excuse me, I DO know I'm born. How could I not?' but it wasn't the right time. And I couldn't exactly say that having a washing machine and two loos isn't really the sort of thing I count as 'lucky'. I can't imagine many girls at school are dancing about the corridors just because they have two loos. A computer for myself and a bit of time to speak to my own dad – now that would be lucky. Still, I knew what she meant because that's the sort of thing Mum always says. Or used to say. That's why it's so awful seeing her like she is now. She either doesn't seem to care at all, or she cares so much she gets really cross and shouts and cries.

So I knew I didn't really have a choice.

Gran carried the bucket into the loo. 'Let's do this now, without your mum seeing, and then you can surprise her. The trick is not to breathe with your nose,' she said.

What was I supposed to breathe with? My ears?

I suppose you'd have thought it was fine, Timmy. I have seen you eat DISGUSTING things out on walks. I suppose for dogs the smell of nappies could be bottled as perfume.

But I am not a dog.

Then, after we'd rinsed the dirty nappies in the

loo, Gran helped me put them in a bucket to soak with water and bicarbonate of soda. So we have got bicarbonate of soda. Though it might feel a bit weird putting the same stuff in my hair that goes in a nappy bucket.

Gran said I have to put the ones from the machine in the tumble drier and then tomorrow after school put the ones from the bucket in the machine.

'Okay,' I said. How could I say 'No'?

I know the nappies are sorted, and Gran was very pleased. But the WHOLE EVENING has gone. I've done no violin practice and no homework. I can't even find my planner. You haven't eaten it, have you, Tim?

I wish I was George from *The Famous Five* and you could sleep on my bed. Actually, I wish I was George from *The Famous Five* and we could run away together and go camping and have adventures instead of going to school.

Or washing nappies.

But I'm not. I'm Anna and I'm not at all famous. Yet.

But The Dominoes are going to be great.

And I've remembered a joke I can tell Mohona and Emma.

What type of dog does Dracula have?
A bloodhound.
So it's not all bad.
Night Night, Terrific And Not So Tiny Tim.
Sleep Well.

I can't sleep because I can hear Jack crying again. I'm so glad you're not a barky dog. You're awake and quietly looking at me and I'm looking at you, and there's nothing we can do. He must be really ill like they say. We've got to get him to America. So that's why I'm sitting next to you downstairs on the floor in the middle of the night having a cuddle.

Thank you, Timmy. You're a great help.

Friday

Chapter Eleven

I found my planner. It was under the bed. I think you might have knocked it out of my bag when you were nosing in it yesterday.

At least you didn't eat it.

I'm feeling pretty heroic, actually. I didn't wait until this evening to finish the nappies. I got up really early and I've sorted them all out already for Mum so she can start to feel better about everything. I took the dry nappies out of the tumble drier and put them in the basket ready for Mum when she comes down, and then I got the rinsed ones that were soaking in the bucket and put them in the machine.

Mum is going to be so pleased when she wakes up. And Gran will be impressed when she comes over tonight, and we can tell Dad when he Skypes and that will stop him worrying about us.

I think hanging my jumper out the window

worked last night. It feels all fresh. I'm glad it didn't rain.

I'd better go, Timmy. You'll have to be quick going out in the garden because I don't want to miss my bus. Mum will take you out for a walk later, I'm sure.

Hi Timmy! I'm back! I'm just sneaking a biscuit while Gran's in the sitting room. I know she's making dinner but I can't wait. She's put the washing machine on. I should have left her a note to ask her to put my uniform in too. Still, I can see Jack's sleepsuits and vests and Mum's pyjamas and dressing gown and towels going round. Mum will be pleased. I think we're getting on top of things.

What's the matter?

Oh, Timmy. It's okay. It's just a firework. I'm not going to leave you alone. I went to the display at the park last Saturday with Mohona and Emma, but Dad was here. He said you were fine. Do you remember when you were a puppy and we played you that CD of noises? It was supposed to help you not be scared of them when you got older. It had fireworks and a vacuum cleaner and even a baby crying. It doesn't seem to have worked with fireworks tonight. But you're very calm when Jack cries.

Come here and I'll tell you about my day. Gran's gone into the sitting room and put on her favourite quiz show and I know she won't want me to talk over it.

Listen to me and not the fireworks. And chew your bone.

Right, firstly I forgot to do my food tech homework. I had to do it in a rush at registration but my yellow pencil broke so I had to finish the cheese in brown. I'm hoping it just looks like it was well cooked, but Emma saw it and said, 'Why have you put chocolate on your pizza?'

Anyway, I gave it in, so at least I can't get told off for it being late. I've decided it's more important to eat pizza than write about it, anyway. I'm sure you agree.

It's okay, Timmy. That's just a rocket. Nothing bad is happening.

So – what else . . . I was lucky in RS because there wasn't time for me to read out my hero homework, so no one knew I hadn't done it. I'm not sure if I want to do it about Prince Rupert any more. I'd have to say about his dog weeing, and I don't know if I dare. It's the sort of thing Adam and Rhys would do and think it was funny and nobody else would but they wouldn't care. Or Rachel Addison could do it and everyone would think it was funny. I don't think I could pull it off.

Have a biscuit.

Adam, Brendan, Ranjit, Wesley and Lottie each chose footballers as heroes. Lottie is the only girl in our class who really, really loves football as much as the boys, and when Adam made a sick noise about hers she nearly hit him. Mr O'Connell got really cross and had to ask people to stop booing every time anyone said which football team their hero came from. He said it was a big relief that Amelia Bakewell chose one of the scriptwriters from *Doctor Who*. That was really cool. Annelise chose J.K. Rowling. I wish I'd thought of her. It was really good. Orla Jones chose her gran, which I am NOT going to tell Gran about. Apparently her gran was a dancer and now runs a pensioners' dance group and they have been invited to dance for the Queen. So that's pretty cool.

Then Lauren went up.

'So she can be bothered to do her homework

sometimes,' Emma whispered loudly. I think Lauren heard but she just carried on.

'I've chosen Lord Shaftesbury,' she said.

'Who's that?' whispered Mohona to me. I shrugged.

'Excellent!' said Mr O'Connell. 'And what can you tell us about him?'

'Um. He was a Victorian MP who stopped women and children working down mines, and children working long hours in factories and up chimneys.'

'Do you have any pictures of him you can show the class?'

'I didn't manage to do anything on the computer, but I've got this book from the library,' said Lauren. She handed it to Mr O'Connell and he held it up for us to see.

'Interesting! And why did you choose him to be your hero? It's very cheering to find someone your age who has chosen a Member of Parliament.'

'It's very weird,' whispered Emma behind us.

Lauren went a bit red. 'I just thought he was interesting,' she sort of mumbled. 'He changed things. He argued with people and he changed the law and changed children's lives. They didn't have to work all the time – they could go to school and things they couldn't do before.'

'Marvellous!' said Mr O'Connell. I could have told her she had said EXACTLY the wrong thing. He teaches us for RS but he mainly teaches politics to Years 12 and 13 and he's MAD about it. 'I can see we have a budding MP in our class. Very good, Lauren. Perhaps you might like to be a member of our lunchtime politics club? It would be lovely to have a Year 7 there for a change.'

I couldn't think of anything worse, to be honest. Lauren didn't look that happy when she sat down. I've never seen her at any lunchtime clubs. She's always in the library. She can't be bothered to join in anything normal.

'He wasn't even a famous MP who's on TV,' said Emma when we were packing up our bags. 'Though even that would have been boring.'

Emma really doesn't like Lauren.

That's just a firework, Timmy. Don't be scared. You should hear Mrs White when she's angry. That's much more scary. I'm so glad I'd got my food tech homework done, even if the cheese was brown, because she was in a bad mood again. She gave Lauren another lunchtime detention.

I looked over at Emma. She looked furious. We were going to have another band practice at lunchtime. Emma had given Lauren one of her 'This is what we are going to do' notes at registration.

I would have felt sorry for her but Lauren really doesn't seem to care. And she just sort of stares ahead and doesn't look upset or anything. She doesn't even try.

'Well, that's just brilliant!' I heard Emma say to Lauren as we were sitting down to watch a film on fast food. 'How can we have a band rehearsal today if you're in another detention? Thanks a lot.'

Lauren didn't even say, 'Sorry'. She just shrugged and went off to sit on the opposite side of the classroom from Emma and me and Mohona.

Which was really rude.

We had our band practice without Lauren, but Emma said she couldn't stand the smell in M1, so we didn't do that much before we went outside and just chatted.

Then after school it turned out Mohona was going to Emma's for tea. I felt a bit left out, but then they said we should meet in town tomorrow and sort out the costumes.

I think the fireworks have stopped now, Timmy.

You've been really brave. You probably only noticed more because Dad isn't here. It's scarier without Dad.

We Skyped Dad after dinner. I told him about our band and he thinks The Dominoes is a good name. I wanted to tell him about doing the nappies, but Mum was next to me and I felt a bit strange because she hasn't mentioned anything about it, so I just said I was helping out about the house. Gran's right. There's no point worrying him. We were all very smiley and chatty and I told him I was going to teach you dancing and he laughed.

I like making Dad laugh.

Secretly I was hoping Gran would tell him what a help I was. She got really over-excited when it was her turn. She practically pushed me off the chair to get to him. Not that she sat down. Gran gets very nervous about talking to Dad on Skype. I think she gets it mixed up with being on television, as if he's interviewing her for the news or something. She practically curtseyed and leaned into the screen and then shouted 'YES' when he asked her if everyone was well. She wasn't herself at all. And she didn't say anything about not being here next week. Or about me doing the nappies either.

'Okay, then. Internet access is a bit patchy here,

but I'll check in as often as I can,' said Dad. 'I must go. Lots of love.' Then the session was over.

And it was funny, but as soon as Dad had gone everything went flat. It wasn't that we got cross or anything, but it felt like when Christmas finishes, or going back to school after the holidays.

'So, I'll be at Edie's until Wednesday but Anna will help out. You'll be fine,' said Gran, almost as if she was convincing herself as she left.

'Yes, Anna and I will be fine,' said Mum.

Saturday

Chapter Twelve

I love taking Emma and Mohona to Buttons and Bows. They really like the little bell that rings when you open the door, and how as soon as you come in you see different colours everywhere. I know you wouldn't, Timmy, because you only see in black and white. But I suppose you smell in colour.

Anyway, even in black and white you could still see all the velvet coats and tweed caps and patterned dresses and vintage handbags and shoes. Gran thinks it's like a jumble sale, but it's really not. It's like an art gallery or a museum – but with things you can pick up and look at, and with clothes you'd actually want to wear. Sometimes Mum would put on music from the 1950s or 60s, and you could see people smiling and swaying a little as they looked through the things. It made her so happy.

Now Matt's doing all the things Mum used

to do. I love his stripy tops and glasses. He's an art student. He has ear piercings and he draws really cool pictures. But he's not Mum. She should be there too. She could bring Jack and he could be behind the counter in his Moses basket and look up at all the ties and hats and he'd probably stop crying. But she says she doesn't want to risk taking Jack in yet.

She was in a good mood this morning before I left, though – she gave me some money to get something nice for lunch. And she said that this afternoon me, you, her and Jack will go and get fish and chips and sit by the beach. We'll take you for a walk and throw you balls and complain and laugh when you get wet and sandy and shake yourself over us. We haven't done that for so long. We've NEVER done it with Jack.

It's funny how most of our lives Jack hasn't been here, and now it's like the rest of our lives never happened.

'Hi, guys!' Matt said when we arrived. Nobody else was in the shop, but even with just us it felt quite crowded. The rails were all jam-packed with coats, dresses, hats and scarves, and rows of shoes were lined up on the floor. Matt was sitting on a stool behind the counter, drawing. He lifted up the piece of paper to show us – it was a cartoon of a dog wearing a trilby and a sign saying fifty per cent off all hats.

'Look!' said Mohona. 'It's cartoon Timmy!' Mohona loves you. She says she wants to come round and help me teach you to dance. Her parents will only let her have stick insects.

'Frankie Santoro is coming to our school on Friday to launch her new charity,' I said. For a moment, Matt stopped drawing, but then he carried on colouring in the dog's trilby with a red marker pen. 'And they want a band to support her, so we're going to audition for it.'

I suddenly wondered whether Matt is still in touch with Frankie. It must be really strange for him seeing his ex-girlfriend on the TV and in the papers all the time.

'I didn't know you were in a band,' said Matt, holding out the poster at arm's length to check if it was finished. You're a perfect subject, Timmy. I once read that golden retrievers are the movie stars of the dog world. I know exactly why. You can look so . . . noble. Especially just before dinner.

Matt's picture is amazing. He put it back on

the counter and signed it with a big squiggly Matt signature. He wants to illustrate children's books. I think he's going to be famous one day. Then that picture of you will be worth millions.

'Well, we want to be on TV, so we were going to start one, and now we have to be in one because Mrs Berlinski is making us,' I said.

'Who's in your band, then?' asked Matt, putting the picture in the window and arranging some hats beside of it. 'Just you three?'

'No, worse luck,' said Emma, trying on a feather boa in front of the mirror. 'We've also got this awful girl called Lauren who can't be bothered to do anything. Mohona sings, I play guitar and Anna plays the violin.'

Matt looked at me. 'What does Lauren do?'

'Nothing. She never turns up to band practice so we're just going to give her a tambourine.'

'Well, she might turn up,' said Mohona, trying to be fair, as usual. 'We haven't practised much, really. She said she could sing. I think we should hear her.' She reached for some long gloves and tried them on. They looked amazing on her. Really elegant.

'She was in detention during our first two rehearsals. I don't think she cares,' said Emma, putting on a hat with a veil halfway over her face. 'And you're our lead singer, Mohona. I don't see why she should just come and take over.'

'So what can I do to help?' said Matt, taking a coat from the rail and putting it on a dummy.

'We need costumes,' I said. 'Can we borrow some for the audition? They need to be black and white.'

'I don't see why not. Do you want to choose some? What about the fourth member? Is she going to try anything on?' said Matt.

'We'll just choose something for her,' said Emma. 'Anna can try stuff on. She's about the same height as Lauren.'

It was weird then, because I suddenly realised that I didn't know what Lauren looks like – I mean, I do generally, but I have no idea what colour eyes she has and I couldn't picture her face clearly, even though she sits behind me every day.

'How's Jack?' said Matt, changing the subject.

I never know what to say when people ask me about my brother, Timmy. So I shrugged. 'He's okay. He's going to see a specialist in the hospital when Dad gets back. They're doing tests. And Mum is starting a Facebook campaign to take him to a doctor in America her friend has heard of.'

Matt nodded. 'He'll be okay, Anna.'

I didn't want to talk about Jack any more.

'Come on! Let's try some outfits!' I said. 'What can we take, Matt?'

'You can have anything apart from the clothes on the mannequin in the window – they've already been reserved,' he said, which was a bit of a shame as she was wearing the most amazing black and white striped Edwardian Dress and a big black hat with ostrich plumes.

Anyway, there were lots of other lovely things and in the end we all looked really good, Timmy. Mohona put on a little black hat called a fascinator and a black boa and a long, white dress that fitted her perfectly. Matt found her some flat, white shoes. Emma had a shorter, black, spangly dress and long, black boots and a wide-brimmed hat, so she looked really sophisticated. I had a black and white polka-dot 50s dress and a pill-box hat. It really does look like a little box. I had black shoes, and I tried on a 1920s straight, black dress, a headband and white shoes with a strap for Lauren.

'Can we put them in the storeroom, Matt?' I asked. 'And collect them nearer the time?'

'Shouldn't be a problem,' said Matt. 'When do you need them?'

'The dress rehearsal is on Wednesday,' said Emma. 'Then we'll ask to keep them at school for the Thursday auditions, and, if we're chosen, until Friday.'

'Are you sure you can collect them, Anna?' said Mohona.

'It's no problem,' I said. 'I'll get them on Tuesday after school.'

'They're wonderful!' said Mohona. 'Thanks so much!'

We posed in front of the mirror and Matt took a photo of us. We looked fantastic! He says he's going to put the picture up in the shop as an advert.

I had forgotten how much fun the shop is. Mum stopped working there last year once she got pregnant with Jack. She said she didn't want to risk anything going wrong, and the doctor said she had to rest. I remember that Matt baked a chocolate cake on her last day and Mum said she was glad she had drunk all of Sandra's terrible-smelling tea because it was worth every disgusting sip to be pregnant again. Not that she would have said about it being disgusting if Sandra had been there. Dad teased her about that.

They were really happy. We were all really happy about Jack.

I've decided I'm going to raise lots of money to get Jack to America. Maybe our band could even release a CD. We could write a song.

We each bought a pancake from the stall in town and ate it on the bench for lunch. Then Emma and Mohona went off to do some shopping. They said they had something they needed to talk about in private. It's too soon for Christmas presents, so it can't be that.

I felt a bit hurt, to be honest. I thought we were going to go round the shops together and try things on. I really want some new jeans. It's no fun trying them on your own. So I came home and Mum said Gran is on her way round again (which is why I am hoovering right by your head – sorry, Tim). The day has been sort of disappearing and I feel a bit miserable suddenly.

But I did have some money left over from what Mum gave me, so I got you a dental stick from the pet shop. Here you go. I bet dentists would love it if people were as keen on brushing their teeth as you are. Maybe they would be if they had human dental sticks – something delicious and crunchy which makes people's teeth clean. Maybe that could be my money-making idea. We can become famous inventors of dental sticks for humans and sell them and make millions of pounds. Then Jack could go to that doctor in America.

I should add it to my list of inventions. I'm not sure where it is, though. I'd also like to create self-writing homework. And self-tidying rooms.

Chapter Thirteen

Gran wants to have a little word with me, Timmy. I hope it isn't another 'nice chat' about nappies. She says Mum has taken Jack out in the pram to get him back to sleep. I thought we were all going to the beach this afternoon.

But when Gran says something you don't really argue. That's why Mum finds her so difficult. When Mum was really sad while she was trying to get pregnant again, Gran told her she had to pull herself together and look after the family she already had.

That made Dad very cross. He didn't speak to Gran for ages, not until just before Jack was born. But it was Mum who said that Dad should try to make it up with her. She said that Gran is old and that she needed to see her son and granddaughter and get to know Jack.

Dad said he would let Gran visit but only on the

condition that she didn't give Mum a hard time. And I think she is trying. You can tell she still thinks our house is too full of dreamcatchers and organic stuff she doesn't see the point in, but she doesn't say so. Well, not as much as she used to.

Gran's 'little word' was that she wanted to teach me how to change the beds. Why? Why couldn't she have just gone to Edie's like she said she was? Why did she have to come back and spoil our Saturday and make up new jobs?

'I've just been in your bedrooms and looked at the sheets and they're grey!' she said.

That's a bit of an exaggeration.

Gran says Dad is working hard in a very important job a long way from home and she is worried he was looking tired when she saw him on the computer, and she said that Mum is busy with Jack, and that when she was a girl she used to help her family and she has noticed I don't do any jobs around the house (What? I have only just learnt to do the nappies. What does she call that? AND I hoovered today. And I make tea and sometimes load the dishwasher) and I'm a good girl but I am very untidy and she didn't feel right going off without making sure that the house was fine.

She says I'm a good girl (again) but I shouldn't waste time playing the violin because I've obviously got no talent and it's very expensive for my parents.

And that I should concentrate on my maths, especially after not being very good at maths in Year 6. I'm Year 7 now, Timmy! A lot has happened since Year 6.

And I don't think that's fair about the violin. When I started in September Miss Green said I was very promising. She said my bow hold was good and she thought I had a good ear. But Mum and Jack need to rest a lot. Nobody ever seems to think it's the right time for me to practise.

I think I could be good, Timmy. It's just you can't be good if you never play. And none of you seem to like it when I do.

You're so lucky you can sleep so much. I read somewhere that dogs sleep eighteen hours a day. Not if they've got grans like mine. Gran and I have just taken all the sheets off the beds, and I have to admit that she's right – they aren't very clean. So then she took the washed sleepsuits and towels and Mum's pyjamas and dressing gown out of the washing machine, and she has filled it with dirty sheets and put them on a hot wash and she says she will teach me how to hang them outside as the cost of tumble drying is astronomical. And we are going to need all the money we can if we are going to take Jack to America to see that doctor.

Then Gran and I put fresh sheets and duvet covers and pillowcases on the beds, and they do look really nice. I wish I could get in mine now and go to sleep. Gran supervised me hanging out Mum's pyjamas and Jack's sleepsuits on the washing line, and then she came in and said she was going to teach me how to make a shepherd's pie for dinner (oh NO!) and we have peeled HUNDREDS of potatoes and I want to die.

Gran so far has been shocked that:

a) I think I can play the violin.
b) Violin lessons cost so much money.
c) Our sheets are so dirty.
d) I hadn't noticed that our sheets are so dirty.
e) I've never washed sheets before.

f) I didn't hang Mum's pyjamas on the line properly (trousers go upside down).

g) I didn't know how to do hospital corners on the beds when we made them up together.

h) I had twelve books in my bed when we made it.

i) I don't hold the potato peeler properly.

j) I haven't been taught how to hold the potato peeler properly. She just about managed NOT to say that Mum should have taught me, but I know that's what she means. The funny thing is that she wouldn't expect Dad to be able to use one or teach me how to, even though he is a brilliant cook. He's better than Mum, actually.

k) I don't chop onions up very well.

l) I cried when I chopped onions and didn't know that you should stick a fork in the root and that stops you crying.

m) I have never made shepherd's pie before.

n) I've never mopped the kitchen floor before, and didn't know that I should do it every day.

o) I want to have a break. This is the most exhausting Saturday afternoon I have ever had.

Chapter Fourteen

The pie is ready to be put in the oven, the kitchen floor is swept and mopped and Gran has made us wash up every single thing we used and put it away. But now she wants us to clean the sitting-room windows before Mum comes back. She says it will cheer us all up. It's not cheering me up.

I said we didn't have any stuff for cleaning windows but she says that we can do it with balls of newspaper. That's why I'm in your area, Timmy, looking for newspaper in the recycling bins. It's true you can clean windows with newspaper – I've seen Gran do it in her house. She has loads of tips for doing things with bicarbonate of soda (it's not just for greasy hair – I've got to tell Mohona) and not throwing away things until they have absolutely been used up. She fills up empty shampoo bottles with water and gets enough shampoo for another hair wash, she knits, and she always puts another layer on rather than turn the heating up. And when the toothpaste seems to be empty she cuts along the edge and opens up the tube and there is enough toothpaste on the sides to use again. She loves recycling rubbish.

It's very calming brushing you, Timmy. Sorry I haven't done it for a while. I'm going to take your hair out into the garden and throw it into the air, and the birds will use it for their nests. I saw that on *Springwatch*. Isn't that cool? I love the idea of baby birds in a Timmy nest. I bet they'll feel really cosy.

Did you hear Mum when she got back from her walk? She said the house looked fantastic. She said she'd had a lovely time because Jack fell asleep in the pram so she went and had a coffee in the tearooms and Jack hadn't woken up. She was so pleased and she gave me a big hug.

'I taught Anna how to cook this shepherd's pie. She has tidied the kitchen, and washed and changed the sheets,' declared Gran. 'She's a big girl now. She can be more help around the house.'

'It looks delicious, Anna. Thank you so much,' said Mum, and she reached across and took my hand. I don't remember when she last touched me like that. It made me feel great and like I wanted to cry at the same time. It was worth being so tired just to see Mum smile. She looked really pretty. Her eyes were sparkling like they used to. My cooking and tidying seemed to have really cheered her up.

Mum said, 'Anna, let's take Timmy out for that walk. Just you and me. While Jack is still asleep. You don't mind watching him, do you, Gran? I'll keep my phone on in case you need me to come back but I think he'll sleep through now for a while.'

Don't mind? Gran looked like she'd been given a prize.

So that's why we went to the beach after all. It was already getting darker and a bit cold, but I loved the way you didn't care, Timmy. You aren't scared of anything. It was empty apart from a few other dog walkers. You met dogs you didn't know but you just ran up to them, wagged your tail and showed them that you were friendly. You are the most positive person I know.

I want to be like you.

While you were running about and we were throwing balls for you, Mum told me she had a really good feeling about this Facebook campaign and Jack getting better. She put her arm round my shoulders and gave me a hug. I leaned into her. It was brilliant just walking along the beach with her, hearing the sea and the birds and seeing the sky get bluer and redder as the sun started setting. I loved the way the clouds lit up from underneath. Then we had to call you back to put you on the lead, because even though you are so golden it was getting hard to see you at a distance in the twilight.

Gran went off home, and Mum said why not save the shepherd's pie for next week and freeze it. So Mum gave me some money for the chippie and I bought us fish and chips for supper.

I think you liked watching *Oliver!* with us on DVD. We sang 'Consider Yourself' to Jack. He waved his little arms and Mum was smiling and everything was turning out fine again. I suddenly thought, yes, we ARE going to get along.

Jack is going to get well, and Mum will not be so tired.

Dad will be back in less than a week.

And Timmy – you're so much better than Bill Sykes's dog.

Monday

Chapter Fifteen

Mum is upstairs sitting on the bed, crying.

She was very quiet, probably because she didn't want to wake Jack. Once Jack starts crying there's no competition. He might not be loud, but he knows how to keep going.

'Sorry, Anna, I'm just being silly. Don't miss your bus. We'll be fine,' she said, trying to smile. I gave her a hug. I was panicking a bit because, honestly, Timmy, if Mum isn't fine I'm not sure what to do. I can't exactly stay home. It's Monday.

How can things change so much in a day? Mum was fine yesterday, wasn't she? More than fine. Me and Gran cleaning the house on Saturday made her so happy. She was even up before me on Sunday and let me sleep in. Then she said she fancied driving to the new big shopping centre and having milkshakes, so we did, and she bought me some jeans and a top and boots. So I'm glad I didn't get them with Emma and Mohona. And we had lunch out and I told Mum about my play and she said she'd love to see it. And we got Jack a teddy and new vests. It was brilliant.

I'm sorry we couldn't take you. We did buy you some toys, though. And we took you for a walk on the beach, and then Mum said she felt like watching a film and cuddling on the sofa with me and Jack. And I didn't want to spoil things by even thinking about homework – it was just so great Mum being back to normal. So we had the shepherd's pie and Mum made popcorn and we ate it in front of the TV and watched Mum's *Downton Abbey* box set. Three episodes back to back. And then hot chocolate and bed.

Yesterday was a brilliant day.

I don't understand.

I've poured Mum some orange juice and made her some toast and I'll bring it up on a tray.

She wasn't crying any more. So that's good. She wants to watch another DVD tonight and she says she's going to get us some fish and chips again for a treat. I didn't remind her that we had them on Saturday. And

I don't know how I can get all my homework done if we watch TV again.

I don't have time to have a shower now. I've put some nappies in the tumble drier in case Mum runs out. I still haven't managed to wash my uniform. I forgot all about it yesterday. Luckily once I've got it on I don't think anyone can see how dirty my blouse collar is, and I think putting my jumper out of the open window again really helped. The dog hairs haven't completely gone and I don't know where the Sellotape is, but I don't have the time to look because . . . Oh no!

1. I haven't done my physics homework and I don't know where my physics book is.

2. It's geography after break and I haven't done that either.

3. I haven't washed my PE kit.

4. I think I've got a maths test but I can't remember what it is on.

I'm doomed.

I ran as fast as I could and got to the bus at the same time as Stinky Brown. Luckily he doesn't catch the bus every day. Someone said he often just hangs around town and doesn't go to school at all. I remember him from primary. I don't remember him being stinky then, but he is now. If Gran thinks our sheets are grey, she should see his shirt. I don't know why he doesn't try to look better. He doesn't always catch our bus, but when he does someone always makes a sound like they are going to be sick, or someone down the back shouts about opening the windows. And you always hear the word 'Stinky', like a code. Operation Stinky. Emergency. Close all nostrils. I had to stand next to him. Kirsty Stewart and her friends were making sick noises, but he looked straight ahead and ignored them. I just tried not to breathe.

I feel a lot better about Mohona and Emma going off on Saturday. Mohona even had a present for me. She said she saw some perfume on a two-for-one offer, and she bought one and got one for me. I hope Emma doesn't mind me getting a present and not her. It's quite strong – even I can smell it. I squirted a bit on at registration. It really cheered me up.

Mr Hawkins gave us the maths test. I have absolutely no idea what most of the questions meant so I'm not too sure if I gave the right answers. But I had a good go.

Physics was awful. Mr Peterson was in a really bad mood. He strode around and opened all the windows for fresh air so we were all freezing and he took two marks off our whole class score because I didn't have my book or my homework. Which meant that Emma was a bit cross with me because she is very keen that our form wins the Inter-form Physics Challenge.

'Anna, you're going to let us all down if you don't focus a bit more,' Emma said at break.

So I'm going to focus.

Luckily I had enough time to plan most of my poster for geography in break, and I finished it off on my lap in the RS cover lesson when we were supposed to be watching a DVD on saints. I did see that St Francis tamed a wolf, Timmy. You'd have liked him. I really like it when we watch DVDs in lessons. They should do that more often. Then in geography my poster about green living went down really well. I even used Gran's tips about cleaning windows with newspaper. Mr Cassidy was very pleased and demonstrated it as a good example to the class and gave me a merit mark, which I can't wait to tell Mum about.

He opened all the windows too. The teachers seem to be very keen on fresh air at the moment.

At lunch we had band practice. Emma told Lauren about it at break, but she didn't bother to turn up. We listened to Dylan's song again and we found the words on the internet. Mohona's voice is okay, but quiet, and Emma was a bit slow changing chords, and none of us can work out why the notes on the violin still don't sound like the song Mohona is singing. They sort of clash. I don't really understand about key signatures, but it might be something to do with that. There's definitely something wrong.

Mohona says we need to practise more, but she and Emma seemed quite keen to cut the session short.

Miss O'Reilly was a bit cross I hadn't washed my PE kit. I wasn't the only one, though. Lauren hadn't done hers either. I'm not that good at hockey but I like it. It was great, just running and trying to hit the ball and getting it off people and pushing it forward. So much simpler than everything else at the moment. I think all this running for the bus is making me faster.

Oh, and Kirsty Stewart and this old lady had a big row at the bus stop about getting on the bus. It was really crowded and Kirsty Stewart had to stay behind on the pavement and she looked really cross. It was really busy all the way home, and I could hear people saying 'Stinky', so I held my breath. Then when I got off the bus, Stinky Brown was already on the other side of the road, kicking a ball. How did he do that? Perhaps he's had practice sprinting for the bus as well.

Did you like the fish, Timmy? I'm sorry I didn't bring you with me, but I didn't know what I would do with you when I went to the shop. Mum didn't really feel like going out as she was still in her nightie and Jack needed a feed so she asked me to go and get them on my own.

I saw Stinky Brown again. It seems like he is everywhere. He had a little boy with him, who looked like a mini Stinky Brown, and they were both kicking a football outside the shop and getting in the way of customers until the fish-and-chip man told them to get lost. I'm glad he did, because I didn't want to get hit by the football coming out.

Mum was dressed when I got back from the fish-and-chip shop and Jack was asleep, so that meant she was feeling a bit better. We took our trays and watched *The Incredibles* together while we ate. Mum smiled when I said the Incredible family were like our family. I know they aren't exactly – but if we count you then there are three children. You're very fast at running, so Dash is definitely your other name, and I've got longish hair. I'm glad Jack doesn't burst into flames, though. I was a bit sad Mum didn't enjoy it more – I kept looking over and she had her eyes closed a lot of the time. It wasn't as good as watching *Oliver*.

Anyway, then I said I'd make the tea. While the kettle was on I quickly did the nappies (SO disgusting!). Then I did the tea, but when I brought the mugs in Mum was on the phone to Dad. She passed it to me and went to change Jack's nappy, because he'd just woken up and started crying.

'Hello, Anna! How's Mum?' asked Dad, even though he had just spoken to her. 'I couldn't get through on Skype.'

'She's fine. She's just upstairs doing Jack's nappy.' I knew what he wanted to hear. I could hear Dad's relieved sigh. 'I got a merit mark in geography. We've just had fish and chips and watched a film,' I said. I didn't say anything about Mum having her eyes closed through most of it.

'Anna – do you think you could do an online grocery shop? I just want to make sure your mum's not stressed, and I thought if we just topped up on everything it might help. If you get a piece of paper I'll tell you the password and how to order stuff. My card details are already stored.'

I felt really proud. I've never done online shopping before. And Dad told me that the password for the account is *lizandannamygirls*. That makes me feel all funny inside.

'You're a star. I love you, Anna,' said Dad.

'I love you too,' I said.

When Mum came down she went into the kitchen with another dirty nappy. I felt a bit upset she didn't say anything about how amazing it was that the bucket was empty. Then she suddenly got sad again.

I don't really know what to do, Timmy. I'm so glad you're here. Have a chew. We haven't got many left now. I'd better get some more.

I've done the shopping. I've booked a slot for Thursday night, just before Dad comes home. I went on favourites and I doubled everything so it will last longer and nobody will have to worry about shopping for ages. I got loads of two for one offers and bargains – it was great. I got lots of dog chews and dental sticks and fruit and vegetables and toilet rolls and frozen dinners, so if Jack keeps being ill and Mum's so busy and Dad goes away again I won't have to keep cooking meals. You can have too many shepherd's pies and even fish and chips stops being a treat if you eat it every night.

Tuesday

Chapter Sixteen

Morning, Timbo. Mum and Jack aren't down, so I'll be your breakfast waitress today. And I'll sweep the floor. You can go out in the garden while I do that. I'll put the nappies in the tumble dryer. Then I'll have breakfast and make my sandwiches.

Bye, Timmy! Be good!

I can't talk about what happened at school today, Timmy.

What Mohona and Emma said.

Even though they meant to be kind.

I can't even talk about it to you.

I just want to put my arms around you and cry and cry and cry.

I don't want to go in the sitting room. Mum's on the phone to Sandra talking about America and Jack, and now she's saying she wants us all to go and live there.

How can we all go to America? What would happen to you?

I'm not leaving you, Timmy.

I want to go upstairs and get out of these horrible, stinky, clothes. The uniform that has been getting smellier and smellier this past week and nobody told me. Nobody.

Until today.

'Can you come to the music room at break?' Emma said, once we had finished the chemistry test I'd forgotten to revise for. I don't think I've done very well. I don't care, though. I know now there are worse things than chemistry tests.

'Okay,' I said. 'But is there time to do any practice?'

'We just want to tell you something,' said Emma.

So I got there and we were all sitting there in the room, and I was wondering what they were going to tell me. Mohona looked very nervous and kept tapping a drum with her hand until Emma looked at her.

'Anna,' said Emma. 'You know the teachers keep opening the windows?'

'Yes,' I said. I couldn't understand what we were talking about.

'Well, it's because of you. You smell.'

'Sorry?' I said.

'You smell, Anna. It's been getting worse and worse. Now it's really bad. Can't you smell yourself? Look, we love you, but it can't go on like this.'

I started to cry and Mohona put her arm around me.

'Why didn't you tell me?' I said.

'That's what we had to talk about on Saturday,' said Emma. 'About how to tell you. We thought maybe if we gave you the perfume then you'd sort of get the hint and wash your clothes.'

'And I thought it might help,' said Mohona quickly.

'Yeah, but putting perfume over a bad smell doesn't fix it. My mum told me that. The only thing that works is being clean and having clean clothes,' said Emma. 'Hasn't your mum noticed how bad you smell?'

It was so hard to hear those words, Timmy.

My best friends were telling me I smelt. That

other people had noticed too. Everyone, except my mum.

All she notices is Jack.

I want to put all my horrible, stinky clothes in the washing machine, but Mum has already filled it with more sleepsuits. She's not too tired to do Jack's clothes. They are going round and round and round and round and they will never ever stop. There will never be room for my clothes. Only Jack's.

And in my room there are more clothes to wash. And my PE kit. I'm going to get it all and put it in a bag and I'm going to get some money from Mum and find a launderette and I won't come back until my clothes are clean.

I never want a day like today again.

Chapter Seventeen

I had a shower and got dressed and went into the sitting room, where Mum was sitting looking at Jack.

'I need to go to the launderette,' I said.

'Sorry?' said Mum. She looked up and frowned at me, not crossly, more like I had woken her from some sort of dream. Like she'd forgotten I existed for a few minutes.

'I've got to go to the launderette. Now,' I said loudly. 'I've got washing to do and there's never room in the washing machine.'

She shook her head as if she couldn't quite make sense of what I was saying. Like the only words she could understand were about doctors and hospitals and America and Jack.

I tried again.

'My uniform needs to be washed and the washing machine is full. I want to go to the launderette.'

'I don't know. Will you be okay on your own?' said Mum, biting her lip the way she does when she is worried.

I didn't look at her. I felt like I was on my own anyway.

'I'll be fine,' I said. 'I got some money from your purse. Please can I go now?'

I could see Mum looking at me as if she wanted to say something, but I didn't want to look back at her. Then Jack started crying. Mum sighed.

'Sorry, Anna, I've got to sort him out,' she said. 'Are you sure you've enough money?' I nodded. 'Well – I suppose it's a good idea. Well done, Anna. That's very . . . mature.' I could tell from the way that her voice was wobbling that she was getting upset and was feeling really bad about herself, but I still didn't want to look at her.

She didn't argue or try to stop me, even though she must have known I didn't know where the launderette was. I just walked out of the room.

I had so many things to wash. In the end I got my wheelie suitcase out of the bottom of the wardrobe and shoved all my horrible, stinky, dirty clothes in it. I looked up the nearest launderette on Google and printed out street directions, the way Dad prints out directions when he's driving off to do one of his stupid interviews.

I was so angry, Timmy. Being angry was the only way I could be brave enough to get to the launderette. If I let myself think for too long, I knew the anger would all turn into tears, and I didn't have the time. I had to get this done. I couldn't bear having dirty clothes one minute longer. So I kept being angry, I didn't let myself cry and I pulled my suitcase down four streets and across a busy main road until I got to the launderette.

'Do you know how to use the machines?' said the woman sitting at the back behind a counter. I shook my head. She sighed. 'There are instructions on them – it's pretty easy to work out. Where's your washing powder?'

I told her I hadn't got any. And then she asked if I had the right change and I said I didn't have that either. So she told me to give her the fiver I was holding and she fished around under the counter, then handed me a bag of change and a cup of washing powder. 'Use a thirty-degree wash. Then the dark colours won't run on the white. And use a medium-hot dryer.'

The woman walked off into a side room and left

me there and suddenly going to a launderette on my own seemed like a really big thing after all. I hadn't even brought a book. I just hoped there would be magazines, like at the doctor's.

Chapter Eighteen

The launderette was nearly empty. There was a man in one corner unloading his washing. He looked a bit like a wanted man from the news or something. That made my heart thump a little bit, so I went to a machine on the other side, in between a couple of girls who were waiting for their washing and talking about uni and some lecture they thought was boring, and some little kids and their mum.

I read the instructions on the machine and opened the door and put my uniform in. My hands were trembling a bit, but I just kept remembering Emma saying, 'Anna, you smell,' and Mohona looking really sorry, and I thought how my own mum hadn't noticed, and how bossy Gran was, and how Dad kept going away, and that made me angry enough with them all to not give in. I found where you put the washing powder and the coins, and pressed the button. When I heard the machine switch on and the sound of the water rushing in to clean the clothes, I felt so relieved I wanted to cry. It was so lovely seeing my uniform rock back and forth and the suds start to gather against the window, and I knew all the time the smell would be going, the dirt washed away. I could have watched it like a TV.

Which is what the boy next to me was doing. He wasn't a toddler or anything. He looked quite old, like seven or something, but he was just sitting on the floor watching the clothes go round and round like it was the most interesting thing ever.

Suddenly I had something plonked on my lap. I looked down to see a pile of books and then a tiny girl climbing up next to me on the bench. It was quite an effort for her, but she did it.

'Can you read me a story, please?' she said.

'Molly!' said her mum. 'Leave that girl alone! Come back here this minute.'

'It's okay, I don't mind reading her a book,' I said to her mum.

Only it wasn't a mum.

It was Lauren.

I felt really awkward.

The first thing I noticed was that Lauren didn't

look all that pleased to see me. The second thing was that she'd been organised enough to bring her school books with her, and I wished I'd done the same.

But the third thing I noticed was that there was a girl of about nine sitting next to her, and she had her homework book on her lap too, and there was nobody else.

'Lauren. You said you'd help me,' said the girl, pulling at Lauren's sleeve. 'I can't do this.'

'Read me some books. Peease,' said Molly at the same time, pulling at my sleeve.

'Molly!' said Lauren.

'No, honestly, it's okay,' I said. 'I'd like to. I haven't got anything else to do.' I looked over at Lauren's lap. She'd brought her English homework. I'd forgotten it. It was about Dickens and *Oliver Twist*.

'Laurennn! You've got to help me with my maths, or Mr Maynard will get cross again with me,' said the older little girl again, and she started coughing.

I felt a warm body climbing up on to my lap and the book pile slid on to the bench. Molly was very determined.

'Read,' she ordered me, picking the top book and pushing it up into my face.

'Honestly, I really haven't got anything else to do,' I repeated to Lauren. 'I'd like to.'

Lauren frowned. She looked as if she wanted to say no, as if she would rather anyone but me was there. We weren't exactly friends, after all. But then she looked over at Molly and you could see her imagining the fuss if she got her to get off my lap, and the girl next to her pulled at her sleeve again.

'Please, Lauren.'

'Thanks,' she said, but not really catching my eye, and then she got on with explaining the maths to the other girl, who I gathered was called Emily, and who seemed to be torn between worry about this Mr Maynard, panic about fractions and having loads of coughing fits.

I tried not to listen to Emily's wails – 'But WHY is one third the same as .333? I don't understand!' – and got on with reading Molly this really cool book about a dog in a beret and his friend who is a sock. It was good putting off having to talk to Lauren, to be honest. I'd never thought about Lauren having sisters. And it was strange but lovely sitting in the launderette holding this warm toddler and feeling her hair tickle my cheek as we looked at the pages together. She pointed out the pictures with her chubby little fingers and said, 'Doggy Claude!' and, 'Bobblysock!' very excitedly as she wiggled about on my lap. I wondered if Jack would be like that when he got older. I hoped so.

'That's my book about Claude and Sir Bobblysock,' said a voice from over our shoulder. It was washing-machine boy. I realised he must be Lauren's brother. He even looked like her.

'It's okay, Tom, Molly is just borrowing it,' said Lauren, looking up from Emily's book.

'But she didn't ask. It's rude not to ask,' said Tom, and reached over and took it from me before I realised what he was doing. Then he went and sat back down in front of the washing machine with the book, while Molly, after a shocked moment, opened her mouth and began to howl.

'Shh, shh,' said Lauren, coming over and taking Molly, whose face was VERY red and whose cries were VERY loud. 'He doesn't mean it. You know what Tom is like with his books.' But Molly kept yelling and Lauren looked really tired.

'We haven't got a mum,' said Emily chattily to me. 'She's dead. That's why Lauren has to look after us all the time. Because Dad has to work when his boss says or we don't have any money. And then we wouldn't have a house or anything. So if Tom gets upset when Dad has to work late we take him to see the machines. The lady lets us. Because our mum is dead.' She made her eyes really big then and dramatic. She didn't seem too upset really, but Lauren looked really stressed. I could tell she didn't want Emily telling me all these things but she didn't have time to stop her because Molly was making so much noise.

I felt really sorry for Lauren and cross with Tom for taking the book. He was just sitting in front of the washing machine, hands over his ears so he couldn't hear Molly, holding his book and rocking back and forth.

I could see the university girls and another lady loading her machine turn round to stare at us, and Lauren looking worriedly at Tom, whose rocking was getting faster and faster.

'We're going to have to sing, Lauren,' said Emily, very solemnly. 'The doggy in the window. It's the only way.'

Lauren closed her eyes for a minute and sighed, and then, looking straight ahead, as if she couldn't even bear to think about where she was and who was watching, she hugged Molly and started to sing

'How Much is that Doggy in the Window?' with Emily over the noise of Molly's yells.

It was amazing. It was really amazing. Emily's voice was a sweet little girl's voice, and she kept stopping because of her cold, but Lauren's – Lauren's voice was so beautiful. It was just a children's song, but her voice was so strong and musical it seemed to fill the launderette. The uni girls stopped frowning and started smiling, and the lady at the end stopped loading her machine and sat down on the bench to listen, and even the scary man looked over and smiled and stopped looking scary. But most of all, like magic, Molly stopped yelling and cuddled into Lauren. Tom's rocking calmed down and he took his hands off his ears.

The song finished and we all clapped – it seemed like there was nothing else we could do. Emily beamed. Molly, tears and snot drying on her round, red cheeks, had bizarrely fallen asleep. Lauren sat down on the bench with her in her arms.

'I knew that would work,' Emily announced to me, very pleased with herself. 'Tom loves it here with all the machines. But if he gets really cross like that Lauren just HAS to sing to him. That always works.'

'I didn't know you could sing like that!' I said

to Lauren. 'You should be the singer in our band.'

She shrugged, but didn't look at me.

'Here's Dad now!' Emily's face lit up as the door opened and a tall man rushed in.

'Sorry, love,' he said to Lauren. 'He wouldn't let me go. Bad evening with Tom?' he said. She nodded, still keeping her eyes on the ground.

He went over to Tom, and squatted down beside him.

'Hello, mate!' he said gently. 'Let's go home.'

'You were late,' said Tom, but he let his dad take his hand and help him to his feet.

'Daddy, I don't feel very well and I can't do my maths,' said Emily, skipping beside him and sounding very cheered up and sorry for herself at the same time. 'And Lauren was rubbish at helping me.' Lauren's dad laughed a bit sadly and looked over at Lauren, who had got up and was now standing behind him holding a sleeping Molly, Molly's head on her shoulder.

'I'm sure she did her best, Emily pet,' he said and ruffled Emily's hair.

'Bye, Lauren,' I called.

She didn't look back.

To be honest, Timmy, I wasn't surprised.

Chapter Nineteen

I noticed Lauren's English book was still on the bench, and ran after them.

'Wait! You forgot this!'

They all turned.

'That girl knows Lauren,' said Emily. 'She read a book to Molly. When I was coughing really badly and Lauren was trying to tell me about maths.'

'Thanks for that,' Lauren's dad said to me. 'Do you go to Bekesbourne High too?'

'Yes,' I said. 'I'm in Lauren's form.'

'Are you Emma or Mohona or Anna?' asked Emily, as if I was famous or something.

'Anna,' I said, feeling a bit weird. Lauren didn't look at me. She seemed to be very busy adjusting Molly in her arms.

'Well, bye, then,' I said and turned and ran back to the launderette.

'Your friend has got an amazing voice!' said one of the students as I got back to my machine.

'Yes, yes she has,' I said.

My washing was finished. I felt ridiculously proud that I had done it. I had managed to get my uniform clean by myself. I opened the door and pulled the clothes out into my bag, then loaded them into a tumble drier, fed in the coins and switched it on. I found a magazine that someone had left behind and tried not to worry about the homework I hadn't done yet. If only I had been organised enough to bring it with me like Lauren. Not that it had helped her, what with Emily and Molly and Tom. No wonder she doesn't get her homework done much.

When my washing was dry I loaded up my suitcase with my lovely, hot, clean clothes and trundled it home.

I don't know how I feel now. There are so many things to think about:

1. Lauren. I didn't know her mum was dead and she has to look after her little brother and sisters. I suppose she has used up all her niceness on her family by the time she comes to class and meets us.

2. And we're not exactly nice to her. The teachers

give her detention and we say she can't be in our band.

3. She should be in our band. Her voice was so amazing. I've got to tell Emma.

4. But I don't want to talk to Emma. Or Mohona. I don't want to see them again. I thought I'd feel better once my uniform was clean, but I don't, because I have to go in again tomorrow for the dress rehearsal and I won't be able to forget what they told me. About me smelling.

Wednesday

Chapter Twenty

I'VE FORGOTTEN THE COSTUMES.

I meant to go to the shop after school yesterday but I completely forgot. I just wanted to get to the launderette.

I wish you had given me a secret signal or something when I was talking to you. I bet Timmy from *The Famous Five* would have reminded George. Although I can't imagine George in a dress. Or a band, really.

I'd better text them to warn them.

SORRY. FORGOT 2 COLLECT COSTUMES LAST NIGHT.

Mohona's texted back.

Don't worry

And Emma.

:(

Emma's not really a morning person. Or an

it's-okay-to-forget-costumes-we-need-for-a-dress-rehearsal sort of person.

Mum's not up again.

So – you've got clean water. You've had breakfast and you've been out in the garden. Stay and sleep until Mum comes down.

Lucky Tim.

I've got so much to tell you. So much has happened today.

I walked into school and as soon as I saw Mohona by the lockers I remembered. Food tech. Fruit salad. Mrs White. I felt sick.

'Mohona,' I said. I could feel myself going red. 'I'm so sorry. I've forgotten . . .'

'It's okay, Anna. Mum gave me too much again.' Mohona smiled and looked at me closely. 'Are you okay?'

'I'm fine,' I said. 'Just tired.' I couldn't bear her to start talking about yesterday. I just wanted us to pretend it had never happened.

Mohona still looked a bit worried and as if she

was going to say something, but I looked away from her and walked quickly into registration and got very busy sorting things out in my bag.

Luckily Suzi and Wesley were having a big row about rehearsal rooms, and Mrs Berlinski came in and gave us a long lecture about how to behave when camera crews were in the school, so then registration was over and Mohona didn't get a chance to ask me anything.

'I knew Lauren wouldn't be here,' Emma complained as we walked along to food tech. 'I've brought bananas and satsumas but she was supposed to bring grapes.' Emma didn't seem to be thinking about yesterday at all.

'Maybe Lauren's got problems,' I said. I wasn't sure if Lauren would want me to talk about her family. I didn't want to give away her secret but I didn't want not to say anything either.

'Problems!' said Emma. 'What problems? I'm sick of her being my partner.'

I bit my lip to stop myself bursting into tears. What if Mohona was sick of being my partner too?

The trouble is, crying in Mrs White's lessons is like bleeding in water when a shark is nearby. I felt like I was going to be executed. Mrs White would hover over me and tell me off about EVERYTHING and I would get worse and worse. That's what always happens. If you go to Mrs White's lessons feeling bad you will feel a million times worse at the end. She'll make sure of that.

But it wasn't Mrs White.

It was Mr Hawkins.

Who knew maths teachers could cook? And I needn't have worried about the ingredients, because just after Lauren came in, late, he said, 'Everyone needs to get their ingredients out now. But I've got a few spares here – lots of grapes and bananas if anyone needs them.'

Brendan and Lauren both went up, and you could see how relieved they felt when they went to collect them and brought them back to their places.

Mrs White would have killed them. She would have killed us.

Mr Hawkins put on some classical music and mostly left us to it. It was really nice, but I still felt a bit funny and sad. I kept worrying Mohona felt the same way about me that Emma feels about Lauren, but I didn't want to ask her in case she said, 'Yes'.

And I knew I was wearing clean clothes and

everything. I knew there was no way I smelt, but I just wanted to keep asking Mohona and Emma, 'Do I still smell? Can you smell me?' but I just couldn't. I actually don't think Emma was thinking about it any more. I think she just thought it was sorted and we should move on. That's what she's like. Besides, she was busy being cross with Lauren.

So as soon as food tech ended I put the spare bowl Mr Hawkins had given me in the fridge and told Mohona and Emma I had to go to the library to do some work. It was true. I still hadn't done my heroes essay. There was hardly anybody there, only Lauren was sitting at a desk writing something. I went up to her. I knew what I had to say and I wanted to get it over with before I chickened out, so it just came out in a bit of a blurt.

'I wanted to say what a brilliant singer you are, Lauren. You should be singing in our band. I'm really sorry you're not.'

Lauren looked startled for a moment, but then she shrugged.

'What are you doing?' I said.

'Maths.'

'Me too. And I've still got to do my RS thing about a hero,' I said.

'Quiet, girls!' said Mrs Jones, tidying up the books, although really it was only me talking.

The bell rang.

'Isn't it time to go to the dress rehearsal now?' said Mrs Jones as she left the library.

Year 7 periods two and three were cancelled so we could have dress rehearsals for the auditions tomorrow.

'Are you coming?' I said. "We don't have the costumes but I think we're supposed to get on stage to check microphones and things.'

Lauren frowned. 'Not much point, is there? I want to catch up on work and I'm not really part of your band. Emma's made that clear. I'll stand at the back and shake a tambourine tomorrow.'

I felt really bad. I should have said something to Emma and Mohona.

'Well, bye, then,' I said.

Chapter Twenty-one

I think we spent too much time in our rehearsals complaining about Lauren (Emma) or talking about Dylan Williams (Mohona) or about how amazing our costumes were (me) and not enough time practising the song.

We thought we knew the song and we'd be fine, but when we got on stage we discovered that my violin sounded really scratchy, Emma's guitar was out of tune and when she tried to tune it a string broke, and when Mohona sang into the microphone she got really startled and forgot the words and looked like she was going to cry.

'Thank you, girls. Maybe a little more work needed before the auditions tomorrow,' said Mr Hawkins, who was marking books at the front. 'I'm sure you'll be fine. Next please.'

'Rubbish,' Suzi Lyons coughed into her hand when we got off the stage.

'Dress rehearsals are meant to go wrong!' said Emma.

'You can't call that an anything rehearsal,' said Suzi scornfully. 'And it didn't sound anything like "Loving You". Unless Dylan Williams has turned into a strangled cat.'

'More like "Hating You",' said Brendan, and Suzi, Caitlin and Tanesha burst out laughing. Pathetic.

Then it was their turn and they did a cover of one of Frankie's own songs, 'Never Let Me Go', and I have to say, Timmy, although I really don't want to, that they were good. Who knew Brendan had such a great voice? And they weren't in costumes, but they did look pretty amazing in their own clothes. Sickeningly so.

'We haven't got a chance,' said Mohona, after we heard them.

'It would have helped if you had at least remembered our costumes, Anna,' said Emma, and stomped off.

'Don't worry, Anna,' said Mohona sadly. 'It

wouldn't have made any difference even if we had worn them.'

Mohona and I went to lunch together. Emma took her sandwiches with her to hockey practice and she was going to meet us for the choir rehearsal. I was quite glad I didn't have to sit through lunch with her because she was so cross with me.

'We just need a bit of practice,' I said, trying to cheer Mohona up. 'Emma's right – dress rehearsals are meant to go wrong. Mum always says that.'

'There isn't any time left to practise! I'm going to die on that stage tomorrow.'

Mohona looked so sad, and I thought about how kind she always is and how really, really, REALLY terrible she was at singing on her own on that stage.

'I know someone who can save our band,' I said.

'That's so awful,' said Mohona, after I'd finished telling her. 'Poor Lauren. No wonder she can't get her work done. I feel terrible about how we've treated her.' Even though she hadn't really been awful to Lauren at all. Not like Emma.

'I think we should ask her to sing in the band,' I said.

'Will it look like we're only wanting to be friends and asking her to be the lead singer tomorrow because she has a good voice?' worried Mohona.

'It might,' I said. 'But I think we should try. And she is SO good. If we have her AND the costumes, we're in with a chance.'

So we went and found Lauren, Timmy. She was in the library, and we had to whisper.

I could see Mohona plucking up her courage. 'I hope it's okay, but Anna told me about your mum, and all the stuff you have to do,' she said nervously. 'And we're both really sorry about the band practices and everything.'

Lauren looked at us. She didn't say anything. She looked at me and then she looked at Mohona, who was looking kind and sorry and a bit desperate.

'And we're not just asking you because we're sorry, but I was wondering, because Anna says you're such a fantastic singer, if . . . if you would join the band properly and wear the costume we chose for you and sing with us tomorrow?' said Mohona. 'I am really, truly terrible and Anna says you are brilliant. We so need you, Lauren.'

Then something wonderful happened, Timmy.

'Okay,' said Lauren. She even smiled a bit.

'Hooray!' said Mohona.

'Would you girls BE QUIET,' said Mrs Jones crossly.

'Sorry,' I said. 'We're going to choir now. It isn't Lauren's fault.'

'Girls!' warned Mrs Jones, and Mohona and I ran out.

It will be a while before Lauren really trusts us, I think, but at least this was a start, and we felt glad. Me because I knew what a brilliant singer Lauren is, and Mohona because she wasn't going to have to sing a solo VERY BADLY on stage in front of the TV people.

'What are we going to do about Emma?' I panted as we ran to the hall for choir. 'She still thinks Lauren doesn't bother about anything and she won't listen to me because she's cross with me about the costumes.'

'I'll try to talk to her,' said Mohona as we got to our choir places just in time.

Emma's an alto and Mohona and I are sopranos, so we weren't near enough to whisper to her in choir even if we'd been allowed to. Twisting round to see her and catching her eye, she still looked really cross, and at registration she volunteered to deliver a message for Mrs Berlinski so she managed to avoid us. Then it was hockey, and because she is so good she got put in a different team.

She changed in a separate part of the changing rooms, but she did come over to talk to us when we were dressed again and standing with Lauren.

'I've texted Matt to say we need the costumes tomorrow morning,' I said. 'I'll get them tonight. I promise.'

'You'd better!' said Emma, ignoring Lauren and GLARING at me. 'Bye, Mohona.' Then she just left.

'She's cross,' said Lauren, rolling her eyes. 'Are you sure this band thing is going to work?'

'I'll talk to her,' said Mohona. I think not having to sing has made her feel she can do anything. It's a good job because we had drama last period and Emma joined Annalise and Lottie when she saw Lauren was with Mohona and me, and then she rushed off before we could catch her. When Emma is cross she is REALLY cross. But Mohona still thinks it will be okay.

I rushed back because Mum texted me at school to ask if I could come home straight away and get a pie from the shop on my way. I'm going to put it in the oven and heat up some baked beans in a saucepan for dinner. Mum says she hasn't been well all day and isn't up to cooking tonight. I've got to sort out those nappies too. I'll take you for a walk first but I DON'T want you chasing anything.

Aunty Helen got back from Spain on Monday and she has sent us a DVD and says she'll come and visit soon. She says she thinks you'll appreciate it, Timmy. It's called *Homeward Bound: The Incredible Journey*. It's got two dogs called Chance and Shadow, who is a golden retriever like you, but American. And – listen to this, Timmy – they are friends with a C-A-T, Timmy. Mum says she'll try to come down and watch it while we eat dinner. Watching a film together seems to be the only way to get her to eat her dinner with me downstairs, anyway.

Making dinner and cleaning up took all my evening, so I didn't get time to go and collect the costumes, but it's okay because I've been getting up so early to do the washing that I can get them before school.

I'm so looking forward to Dad coming home on Saturday. Even more than Frankie Santoro coming on Friday.

Thursday

Chapter Twenty-two

Mum was up already when I came down for breakfast. This should have been good because she was dressed and everything, but it wasn't. Her face looked pinched and stressed.

'Anna, please can you come with me to the doctor's?' she said. Her voice was all tight. 'Jack isn't well again. I just want to check him out. I've rung them and they say to come in first thing.'

Jack looked okay to me. He was asleep in his car seat, with his little coat on and not crying.

'Couldn't Gran go with you?' I said. 'She's back from Evie's now.'

'I can't ask your gran. I can't cope with her. She'll say I'm worrying about nothing again.'

'But, Mum, I'm supposed to go to school.'

'I know. I'll write you a letter. I just . . . I just can't risk Jack's health, and I can't do this on my own. You'll give me strength. Please, Anna.'

Mum was shaking. She was putting on her coat already and doing the buttons up wrong.

'Okay, but I'm going to have to go to school afterwards.'

'Just please come now. I'm sorry.'

'Can you ring the school, then?' I said. 'I can't just not turn up.'

Mum picked up the phone and rang the school.

'Hello? Hello? Yes, it's Mrs Taylor here. I'm Anna Taylor's mum − she's in 7B. Yes. I'm taking Anna to the doctor's. She isn't well.'

I couldn't believe it. Mum was lying. Though I couldn't exactly take the phone from her.

'Yes. Yes, I hope she'll be well enough to come in. We'll see what the doctor says. Thank you. Goodbye.'

'Mum!' I said.

'Look, Anna. You have to come with me. I have to have you with me. Dad isn't here. I have to take Jack to be checked. And it's not as if you're doing much this week. It all seems to be Frankie Santoro this, Frankie Santoro that.'

Frankie Santoro! The audition.

'Mum! I haven't picked up the costumes yet and the audition is today.'

'Anna, I can't deal with that. Jack is ill. Please, just have some breakfast and then we'll go to the doctor's.'

'But —'

'Have your breakfast!' Mum screamed at me. 'I can't believe you are being so selfish. Leave it now or we'll be late. Just take a muesli bar or something. Nobody cares about Jack except me and I can't take it any more.'

Did you hear her? It was so horrible. She has never shouted like that. Ever. I don't know what to do. She has stormed off to the car with Jack. I'd better go.

Chapter Twenty-three

Luckily the doctor's isn't far away. I got in the back of the car and stared out of the window. Mum didn't say anything more. She just fussed about with Jack's seat belt and fastened her own and then drove. When she put on the radio it was somebody in the government talking about lots of children playing truant from school. I wanted to tell the person on the radio that I was a child who wanted to go to school but I couldn't. Mum switched off the radio quickly and we drove the rest of the short journey in angry silence. I sent a text to Emma and Mohona.

Am at doctor's. Will bring costumes.

When we got out, Mum took Jack's car seat and strode ahead, not even looking at me. She went up to reception.

'Appointment for Jack Taylor and Anna Taylor.'

We sat down. I saw Priya Bennet on the seats

opposite us. She was with a very old Indian lady (I think she was her gran) who was coughing a lot. It seemed funny Priya wasn't at school, although when you are in sixth form you get lots of free periods. We sort of smiled at each other, but there was nothing to say really. She'd picked me out of a luggage rack and she was going out with Emma's brother and was head girl. I was in Year 7. That's about it really.

The doctor called us in. She wasn't our usual one, Mohona's mum. This doctor looked really young.

'So, how can I help you today?' she said.

'Anna isn't herself. She says she has a sore throat,' said Mum. 'And I want you to look at Jack. I'm really worried about him.'

'Okay. Let's look at Anna first. I'll just examine your throat, if I may.' It was so embarrassing, Timmy. I had to open my mouth and let her look into it, and let her feel my neck, and I found myself even trying to look ill. I don't know why. I just didn't want it to look as if Mum was lying. I almost started believing it myself.

'Well, there are no signs of any serious problem, and no actual redness,' she said very politely. I found myself blushing, as if I was the one who had lied. 'Any headache? Pains anywhere?' I shook my head. 'Well, let us know if it gets worse, but hopefully you will feel better in a day or so. It's probably just a mild viral infection. There's a lot of them about.' She turned to the screen and typed something in. I wondered if it was *this girl came and lied*, but I couldn't see what she was writing. It was funny, because when I swallowed my throat did really feel sore.

'Could you look at Jack, please?' said Mum. They lifted him out of his car seat and woke him up, which he didn't like. He screamed all the time they were undressing him.

'What specifically seems to be the problem?' she said.

'I just think he seems listless, and I was worried I could see a rash starting,' said Mum.

The doctor listened to his chest and looked at his legs and arms and took his temperature, and all the time he cried.

'He seems fine to me. He has a strong cry, which is good,' said the doctor. 'I can't see any rash that would make me worry. It says here he was premature and you are waiting to see a paediatrician next week about his development, and we are waiting the results of the repeat blood tests you requested, but all the ones so far have been absolutely fine. Certainly he seems to be doing well at the moment. No cause for worry, although obviously don't hesitate to call us if things change.' She smiled at us and as Mum put Jack, still protesting, back into his snowsuit and car seat, she went back to the computer and typed in some more things.

'Thank you very much,' said Mum, in a small, quiet, tired voice.

The doctor swivelled round in her chair and gave us a smile. 'No problem,' she replied as she went back to looking at the screen.

It felt like a long walk past reception to the door.

'I'll take you to school now,' said Mum, in a small voice. 'Thank you for coming.' I didn't feel angry with her any more. It felt like the furiously angry person inside her had gone, and there was just a very little one left in her place. It made me feel more scared, to be honest. Neither of them were the mum I knew.

'Are you okay, Mum?' I said.

'Yes, I'm fine. I'm just a little tired,' she said, putting Jack's seat in the car. I suddenly didn't want to go to school until I knew they were both safely back home.

'I need to get something from my room,' I said. 'Let's go back and then I'll catch the bus in.'

We drove in a different sort of silence. The air wasn't fizzing with anger any more, just heavy with sadness. Jack wasn't crying – he had fallen asleep again. It was strange that the doctor had said he wasn't very ill, but I could see Mum was weeping quietly. Didn't she believe the doctor? I was so glad when we got home and she parked the car.

'Mum – are you sure you're okay?' I said. 'I don't want to go to school if you don't feel well.'

'I'm just tired, Anna. I'm sorry I was so horrible.'

'It's okay, Mum,' I said, giving her a hug. 'You needed to check on Jack. I understand.' But I didn't really, Timmy. And I didn't know what to think about what the doctor had said. If Jack wasn't ill, why was Mum so worried? Why were we doing a Facebook campaign and talking about going to America?

It was lovely to see you when we got back. You wagged your tail so much even Mum smiled a bit. When you were out in the garden I made some sandwiches for my lunch and I made some extra for Mum. Then I made her a cup of tea and she looked a bit better. I found her a TV programme about people building their own houses in a wood, which cheered her up. Jack was asleep in his Moses basket and it felt okay to go. I let you back in and you lay down on the floor in front of Mum and put your paw on her feet. Thanks, Tim.

It was when I was on my way to the bus stop that I remembered the costumes. It was ten thirty by then.

When are you coming? Our slot is at 11:30, texted Emma.

V soon, I texted back.

The bus came and I got on. My tummy felt a bit weird, all tangled up in knots. I felt my heart beating faster as we got to the school bus stop. The bus drew in and stopped and I saw Priya come down the stairs and get off. She must have finished at the doctor's too. She walked past my window but I bent down as if I was getting something out of my bag. I kept bending down until the bus started moving again.

I had done it. I was properly playing truant. I was going into town to get those costumes. I wasn't going to let Emma and Mohona down.

Chapter Twenty-four

I counted the stops until town. Each time the bus stopped I bent down so I couldn't see who was getting on the bus and they wouldn't notice me. I could see from their legs it was mostly elderly people and mums with babies, but I didn't want to look too closely. I just looked out of the window and tried to be invisible. Nobody came to sit next to me, and at last it was the bus stop outside Buttons and Bows.

'Hello, Anna!' said Matt, looking a bit surprised. 'What are you doing here? Didn't you get the costumes? I dropped them off at school reception for you. You didn't collect them on Tuesday and I know you needed them for today, so I rang your mum and told her to tell you that I'd drop them off. Didn't she say?'

'No.'

My phone buzzed. It was Emma asking where I was.

My stomach dipped when I saw the time. Eleven fifteen.

Now I had to get back to school. I wished I'd just got off the bus when I should have. I wished Mum had passed on the message.

'Sorry, Anna. I thought it would help,' said Matt.

'Thanks, Matt,' I said. 'Mum must have forgotten to tell me. I'd better get the bus back now.'

It would have been so much easier if I had the costumes. If someone had stopped me I could have explained. But now I was just coming out of a shop in my school uniform in the middle of the day, and my worst nightmare came true.

'Hello. Shouldn't you be in school?' The police officers were very nice, but very serious.

'I . . . I was just going to collect something for a school concert.'

'On your own? Does your school know?' said the policeman, taking out his phone. 'Shall we phone your mother?'

'No, no, please don't phone Mum,' I started panicking.

'Can I help at all?' It was Mohona's mum, Dr Desai. I was so glad to see her. 'I know this girl. She's friends with my daughter. Anna, are you okay?'

'I just need to get back to school. I thought I was supposed to collect some costumes. I didn't mean to play truant, honestly. They want to phone Mum. Please, please don't let them.'

Dr Desai turned to the policeman and policewoman.

'I'll take her straight there. If you could just let me deal with it I'd be very grateful. There are special circumstances. I'll talk to the school.'

The policeman and policewoman looked at each other.

'Okay. We'll let it pass this time.' They looked at me very sternly. 'But don't let us see you again in town in school hours, costumes or no costumes.'

My legs felt wobbly as Mohona's mum and I set off down the road to the car.

'How lucky I saw you!' she said. 'I heard you and your mum and Jack were at the surgery this morning. You saw Ellie, my trainee.'

I sat in the passenger seat and put on my seat belt.

'Don't worry, Anna, I'll get you back to school and you won't be in trouble. I'll say you were at the surgery and I gave you a lift. We won't say anything about the bit in the middle.'

'Thank you,' I said. I couldn't say any more in case I cried.

'Everything okay at home, Anna?' Mohona's mum looked at me sideways.

I nodded. What was I supposed to say?

'If you ever need any help, if you ever want to talk, please don't hesitate. Is your dad about?'

I shook my head. 'No, he's away, working.' I bit my lip to stop it wobbling. 'He's back on Saturday.'

'Is anyone helping while he isn't there?' she said as we pulled away from the kerb.

'My gran.'

'Good.' She glanced over at me every now and then as she spoke. 'It's not long until Saturday, is it? But, Anna, if you think you might need to talk to someone before then, please ring Mohona, and I can come and help as a friend, not just as your GP. I know how things can get a bit much sometimes.'

She was so kind. But how could I tell her anything when I wasn't sure what I had to tell? What good would it do? I couldn't tell her that Mum had lied about my sore throat. We only had to get to Saturday and then Dad would be home. And I had to get to school to the audition.

'What's the time?' I asked, but just then Mohona's mum got a call on her hands-free. And the car stopped at some temporary traffic lights. There was no way we could get there in time.

Mohona's mum was really good when we got to the school reception. She signed me in and explained that I had just been at the GP's, and then left. I asked for the costumes in a breathless voice and Mrs McNally there seemed to take an age to find them. I looked up at the clock above her desk. Eleven forty-five. Maybe they would let us swap with someone else.

I carried the costumes on hangers over my arms in a slippery tower and ran along the corridor towards our form room, trying to avoid all the people who were rushing past me. It was like the end of term or at a school play. People were dressed up in wigs and fancy dress and carrying guitars. Amelia and Orla were in Irish dancing costumes – I bet the TV crew would interview them. Lauren's costume, at the top of the pile, slid off and fell on the floor.

'Where have you been, Anna?' said Mrs Berlinski, behind me. 'The others are waiting.'

Mrs Berlinski bent down to pick up Lauren's costume and put it on top of my pile and I swayed my way into the room. The noise was deafening. I carried my load of clothes past Suzi, Caitlin and Tanesha and Brendan, who were singing their Frankie Santoro song really loudly and really annoyingly well – with parts and everything – and found Mohona and Emma sitting next to her in my seat. Lauren's and Emma's proper seats were empty behind her.

'At last!' said Emma. 'How long does a doctor's appointment take? Lauren hasn't turned up either.'

'Are you okay, Anna?' said Mohona.

'Er, yes,' I said, but I tried to make my voice sound a bit hoarse so they wouldn't think I had been lying about the doctor's.

'Why did you go to the doctor's anyway?' said Emma, taking her costume from me.

'Um – sore throat,' I said.

'I've got a sore throat too,' said Emma crossly. 'It's not an emergency. We may have missed our slot for the audition. Luckily I think they're running late.'

'Will you be okay to go on?' said Mohona, picking out her hat.

'I . . . I think so,' I said. It felt so strange. I wasn't sure if I was ill or not.

'She doesn't play the violin with her throat,' said Emma.

The violin. I felt sick.

'Oh no. I've . . . I've left it at home. I'm so sorry.'

They stared at me. Emma started to say something but Mrs Berlinski came in.

'Girls!' she said to us. 'Hurry up. You're already late for your slot. And the film crew wants to interview one of the bands. I suggested you because Emma told me you have some wonderful costumes.'

'Thanks, Mrs Berlinski,' said Emma. 'We've got the costumes now but Anna hasn't got her violin. And Lauren hasn't turned up.'

Mrs Berlinski tutted and rolled her eyes. 'Oh, Anna! Well, you're just going to have to miss your slot, then. We can't keep them waiting. Suzi! Can you and Caitlin, Tanesha and Brendan come with me – the film crew can interview you instead. Try to think of something interesting about yourselves.'

Suzi and the others rushed out with Mrs Berlinski looking really excited. Everything was going wrong and I couldn't stop it.

Emma didn't say anything. She just turned and left the room. Mohona followed and then looked back at me as if she expected me to come with them. But I didn't. I just sat in Emma's seat and looked at the costumes, still in their cellophane, lying on the desk.

Chapter Twenty-five

Suzi and the others came back so pleased with their audition and interview. It's just not fair. Apparently the director said they were fantastic singers, which is true. They're just not very nice people.

I wanted to get away from them going on about how brilliant everything was. I didn't want to go to the canteen – I didn't feel like eating anything, and I didn't want to bump into Mohona or Emma. I wanted somewhere quiet. Somewhere away from people singing, or practising card tricks or talking about the auditions. Somewhere away from my two best friends. For the first time I wondered what had stopped Lauren coming to school in the morning and if she felt as bad as me about it. Because I felt so awful. I'd messed up everything.

The library was the only quiet place in the school.

As soon as I pushed open the door I could see it was empty – apart from one person – Lauren.

'Hi, Lauren. I missed the rehearsal too. I had to go to the doctor's with my mum and my baby brother.' She looked at me, but didn't say anything so I just kept talking. 'He has lots of hospital tests and things and Mum gets very worried about him and she wanted me to come with her. But the doctor said he was okay.'

It felt good telling someone. I didn't have to lie about sore throats or anything. I knew Lauren would understand. I know you understand, Timmy. But it's nice to have a human person too.

'Oh, I didn't know you weren't there too,' said Lauren. 'I couldn't come because Tom hurt his arm last night and he's got a sling. He gets really upset when he can't do things, so they said for him to stay off school. I expect Emma's really annoyed but there was nothing I could do – I had to look after Tom till Dad finished his morning shift. His boss is really horrible. He said if he took any more time off he wouldn't use him again.'

Lauren had just said more words in one go than I'd heard her say the whole time I've known her.

When the bell went, Lauren and I went back to class together, but when we got to our seats Emma was in mine next to Mohona, and she was turning her back on me. All our costumes were in a heap across Emma's desk.

'Change of seating, girls?' said Mrs Berlinski. 'Okay, then.' Mohona looked back to catch my eye and I could see she wasn't happy, but we didn't get a chance to say anything because as soon as Mrs Berlinski finished the register she looked at me and said, 'Anna, you can't just leave those costumes there. Take them over to the music department and hang them up with everyone else's. And be quick about it or you'll be late.'

'I'll help,' said Mohona. Emma just stayed put and ignored us. I suppose she didn't feel like carrying a costume she hadn't worn.

Mohona and I gathered up the clothes. I felt really fed up that our lovely costumes weren't going to be used.

'I'm so sorry,' said Mohona as we set off down the corridor. 'I didn't want to change seats. It just sort of happened because Emma was so cross and didn't want to sit with Lauren. She just wouldn't let me explain things to her.'

'I'm really sorry too,' I said. 'I didn't want us to miss the audition. And Lauren didn't want to miss it –

she had to stay off school to look after her brother. It's such a shame no one go to hear her sing.'

'Yeah it is,' said Mohona. 'And she didn't even get to see the costumes.'

'Why don't we show Lauren the costumes after school? We could have a rehearsal just for fun.'

'That's a great idea,' said Mohona. 'And maybe Emma will have calmed down and we can explain things to her.'

We smiled at each other. Then we hung up the costumes in the music department and rushed off to history. Emma ignored us both. I whispered to Lauren about trying on the costumes and she said she could only come for a bit because she had to get home. But I saw she kept smiling to herself (and it wouldn't have been because of the lesson because we were doing the feudal system). On the way to maths, Mohona asked Emma if she'd like to come to the music department after school but she said, 'No'.

After school I saw her walk out the school gates with her big brother. Priya caught up with them and Ramon put his arm round her. I heard him ask Priya how her gran was. Emma walked on ahead of them and Mohona ran after her.

'I'll catch you up!' she called to us.

When Lauren and I got to the music block, the practice rooms were free. We tried on our costumes and looked at ourselves in the full-length mirrors. I thought I looked good, but Lauren looked amazing. She looked so different. I think it was because she looked happy and that made me realise again how she never normally looked happy at school and how mean we had been to her, ignoring her and just thinking she didn't care.

'You should sing something,' I said. Lauren didn't say anything like, 'Oh I can't,' or, 'I'm not good enough.' I suppose if you've had to sing in a launderette to stop your sister screaming and your brother throwing a wobbly you don't get worried about singing in public any more.

So she sang. She was FANTASTIC, Timmy. The practice rooms are great for sound, anyway.

Then we heard the clapping and turned around to see Emma and Mohona.

'That was amazing,' said Mohona. 'I wish Frankie Santoro could have heard it.'

'Who cares about Frankie Santoro?' said Emma. 'That was INCREDIBLE! Lauren – Mohona told me about your mum and everything and I'm so sorry. I've been completely horrible to you. And I'm really sorry I was so mean to you too, Anna. Mohona told me your mum and Jack aren't well.'

That's the good thing about Emma, Timmy – she's very sure when she is right but she is also very sure when she is wrong.

'That's okay,' said Lauren.

'That's okay,' I said.

'So, Lauren – I think you are going to be a superstar and MUCH bigger than Frankie Santoro and I have just decided I want to be your manager! Shall we do some songs? Where's my costume?' said Emma.

Things were back to normal. Actually, they were better than normal because Lauren looked happy from inside out, like a million worries had been taken off her just because she had sung and we like her voice and we know how hard it is for her at home. I'm glad about that, but I'm not sure what good it will do. We can't change anything. I wish we could.

Chapter Twenty-six

I felt happy all the way home about our band and everything, but as soon as I got off at the bus stop I started thinking about Mum and Jack and my stomach started hurting. It was like someone was squeezing my insides really tightly. But when I turned the key in the lock and walked in and you were so pleased to see me, and you licked my hands and rolled over and I tickled your tummy, the pain got a bit less.

Doctor Tim for tums.

I went upstairs to find Mum and opened her bedroom door carefully, but the room was dark, the curtains closed. She was asleep with Jack and she didn't wake up. I closed the door quietly and went to look in the medicine cupboard for some paracetamol, but there wasn't any. Mum always used to have medicines for any emergency. Now there are just some plasters. Gran's come. I told her about my tummy and she tutted when she saw that the medicine cupboard was empty. 'I'll go to the corner shop, you get yourself up to bed,' she fussed.

Sometimes it's nice having Gran here.

The shopping has arrived. The van drove up just after Gran went. I told the driver Gran would be back in a minute. Thanks for going into your area so well and not barking. I saw you wagging your tail as the man helped me unpack the crates and bring lots and lots of bags of food into the kitchen. They covered the whole floor. I knew Mum and Gran would be so pleased when I showed them. We won't need to shop for months.

'Having a party, are you?' he said. I smiled and shook my head. I closed the kitchen door and we went back into the hall. 'Right – now I need an adult to sign for this.'

Luckily Gran came back at just the right minute.

'Could you sign here for the grocery shopping?' he said. 'It's all as ordered. There's been no substitutions.' Gran and the man had a little joke about her signature and then he drove off. It all felt really cheerful.

Gran's hanging her coat up and popping to the loo. I can't wait until she sees what's in the kitchen. She's going to be so pleased.

Where can we go, Timmy?

I don't know what to do.

Our kitchen floor is full of bags and the frozen food is all defrosting and Mum is crying because of all the money it has cost and we need that money to send Jack to America. Gran is on the phone to the delivery people, shouting because she spent the first five minutes talking to an automated voice.

And Jack is crying too now and Mum has gone upstairs to get him.

And I saw shampoo and shower gel in one of the bags and I went to pick them up and Gran shouted, 'Put those down, Anna. They have to go back on the truck,' and she started talking on the phone again. 'Yes, hello. As I've just tried to explain, my daughter-in-law has had a huge delivery from your supermarket costing several hundred pounds her family cannot afford and containing more food than they can possibly store. There's far too much for the freezer, and the vegetables and fruit will all rot, and although there has quite obviously been a mistake I have been told you are refusing to take the food back now that it has been signed for.'

I could hear a little tinny voice at the other end of the phone. Gran interrupted and said, 'No – you listen to me. They've got a sick baby – my daughter-in-law is very worried. Yes, I signed for the shopping. I didn't realise just how much there was ... I don't care what your policy is. They're trying to raise money to send my grandson to America, for goodness' sake. I think this will make the mother very ill. No – you listen to me. My son is a journalist and I will ask him to investigate you ...'

I didn't know what to do. I just put you on the lead and walked out of the door.

I went out the side gate with you while Gran was still arguing on the phone.

No one saw me.

And I've walked down here to the sea because it is big and wet and doesn't care. And now you are sniffing in the rock pools and wagging your tail and you're so far down the beach that you can't hear me tell you how I have been stupid and spent money we needed to take Jack to America, and made Mum ill and let Dad down. I've let everyone down.

And I'm glad you can't hear what I'm saying because I couldn't bear it if you didn't love me any more either.

I didn't know, Timmy.

I wish I had some tissues to wipe my eyes. Now my nose has started running.

My stupid nose. Which couldn't smell what everyone else could.

My stupid everything.

I thought everything had changed. But it hasn't really. It's all horrible and I'm just so tired of it all.

Where can we go, Timmy?

Oh, Timmy – you are so clever. You must have heard me. You've brought me some driftwood and now I know where we can go.

I can't do it on my own any more.

I've tried calling, but I can't get an answer from Aunty Helen, and I've made a mess of leaving a voicemail too – I just kept crying.

And my phone has run out of battery.

I think we'll just go anyway, Timmy. I've got enough money to get us there. I know you've never been on a bus before but it will be fun, honestly.

We'll just wait at the bus stop and get on the bus and then I know the way from the bus stop, and Aunty Helen will know what to do.

She has to.

Come on, Timmy.

Chapter
Twenty-seven

I'm so sorry, Timmy. I didn't think. I didn't think about it getting dark and the headlights being on and dazzling you, and the big bus all lit up, and the noise of its engine, and the other cars and motorbikes, and I didn't think that the sound of the doors opening would scare you so much.

You were too strong for me.

I'm sorry I let go.

It was the worst thing of all, Timmy. As soon as I dropped the lead, you charged off. You ran so fast, away from the street and back on to the beach, and even though I ran after you, you had disappeared. The sky was going from cloudy to black with no beautiful colours in-between. It was cold, and it had started to rain.

I called and I called you, but you didn't come. All I could see was endless wet sand and a grey sea, and a darkening sky and all I could hear were seagulls calling and the sound of buses and cars up on the road above the beach. No waggy tail and friendly licks. No golden you to throw my arms around and listen to me. No dogs at all. Just an empty beach.

And I felt sick.

I closed my eyes and opened them again, as if that would help, but you still weren't there. I thought about when you were a tiny little puppy, and when you were a bouncing Tigger. I thought about you looking all noble when you are waiting for food, and rolling over on your back with your tongue hanging out when you are being silly. I thought about how much I love you, and how much I need you, and I ran up and down the sand in a panic, calling your name.

It got darker and darker. The seabirds were calling and the waves were swooshing in and out, and I was so cold, but I kept hoping I would see a big golden dog running towards me, and everything would be all right.

But it wasn't.

Eventually it was pitch black. I called your name again and again into the darkness and the sound of the sea, but there was no reply.

Then I climbed the steps, and I thought I might see you on the street. The street lamps were on and I walked up and down calling for you. I even asked people at the bus stop and in the shops, but nobody knew anything.

'Go home and tell your mum,' said the man in the newsagent's. 'It's too dark for a young girl to be out on her own.'

So I ran home, and I let myself in and I saw Mum in the sitting room with Gran and before I could ask for help Mum just sort of ran towards me and grabbed me by the shoulders. 'You stupid girl, you stupid girl. Your aunty Helen rang and said you were crying, and I've tried your phone but it's switched off. We've been worried sick. I called your friends but nobody knew where you were. We were just about to ring the police. Where have you been?'

I don't know where it all came from, but I couldn't stand it any more. Instead of crying and saying sorry, I shouted back.

'I HATE YOU. I HATE YOU. I'VE LOST TIMMY. I HATE YOU ALL. I HATE YOU, I HATE GRAN, I HATE DAD. I HATE JACK. I WISH I WAS DEAD.'

Because I did.

Because without you, there was no one for me any more.

And I ran upstairs, past Mum and Gran, and I slammed the door behind me.

And then I started hitting and hitting the door and yelling and screaming, and I ripped up every bit of paper on my desk and I got my shoes and I threw them against the door and I howled.

I pushed my chest of drawers up against the door so they couldn't come in.

And I could hear Gran on the landing telling me to stop it at once, and then I could hear Mum joining her.

And I told her I wouldn't. Because why should I? She didn't stop. She was the one who kept crying, and holding Jack and feeding Jack and talking to Jack and talking about Jack, and insisting on using stupid cloth nappies but never washing them, and nothing I could do could make things right.

I'm supposed to be the good girl, and I've tried. I've really tried. I've tried to be helpful and work hard. I told her I was really excited about the baby coming. I carried his scan with me and showed it to Mohona and Emma. It wasn't only Mum who was sad about Jack coming early and being in hospital.

Dad and I were too. And now Dad is miles away and all he does is tell me to do things and help Mum. And I hardly ever see Jack. First of all he was in hospital and now he is always with Mum or up in his room crying. And Gran comes and plonks him in my lap every now and then and tells me to work hard at school and I'm supposed to be this perfect big sister and I don't know how to be. I don't even know how to be me any more. And when people at school were laughing at me because I smelt, NOBODY in my family noticed. And now I've missed the chance to perform for Frankie Santoro and my friends will never forgive me. But most of all, most of everything, I've lost you.

And I'm hating them both through the door, and if you were here I would tell you: 'No one cares about me. They don't see me, they don't hear me, they don't touch me and they don't even smell me. The only one who loves me is you, Timmy.'

And you aren't here.

Chapter Twenty-eight

Gran and Mum went away. I heard the phone ring and Gran talking. For a moment I thought someone had rung to say you'd been found, but when nobody came back upstairs I knew it wasn't that. You were out in the dark and I couldn't get to you. I cried and cried some more, until I was completely exhausted. I didn't have the energy to shout or hit things or even think any more.

I know now I should have been trying to contact lost dog websites, or phoning the police. Or the vet's. But I didn't think of that. I just curled up in a ball. I'm so sorry, Timmy. I just didn't believe anyone could help me find you. I didn't want to be there. I just didn't want to be – I didn't know how to be – anywhere without you. And I was so, so tired.

I must have fallen asleep because there was a knock on my bedroom door and I woke with a panic.

I swallowed, but my throat was really dry and sore. And I didn't say anything. I didn't want to talk to Mum or Gran. My door opened a tiny bit, as if the person on the other side wasn't sure whether to come in or not.

And through the gap in the doorway I saw Mohona.

'Can I come in?'

I tried to think of something to say, but she pushed the door and it hit the chest of drawers and wouldn't open any further.

'I think you should come downstairs,' said Mohona.

'I lost Timmy,' I blurted out helplessly.

'I know. I rang your mum back to see if you were home yet – that's why we're here.'

'Who's we?' I asked, but Mohona didn't answer. She stood on the landing waiting for me. So I heaved the chest of drawers and opened the door enough to get out.

The hallway was full of people. Mohona's mum, Emma, and her dad, Matt, Mum, Gran – and Lauren and her dad, with Molly, Emily and Tom. And they all had torches.

'We are going to help you find your dog,' said Tom.

Mohona's mum stayed to take care of Mum, Jack and Molly, and the rest of us walked down to the sea.

We reached the edge of the beach and all went in different directions calling your name.

Then, like a miracle, suddenly you appeared out of nowhere. You hurled yourself at me, and you smelt of seaweed and sand and you were wet and cold and so glad to be found.

And running after you was someone else. 'He went right down to the very end of the beach and fell down a deep hole between two rocks, and I couldn't get him out,' came a voice.

It was Stinky Brown, with a little boy beside him. They both looked very tired and cold and wet too. 'I was there with him, me and Jake, and we didn't know what to do. We thought the sea was coming in, and then he heard you all calling and he got himself out.'

'You must have been very frightened all the time you were stuck in that pool. But Stinky Brown didn't leave you.

He shivered. Neither he nor his brother were wearing much – they didn't have thick coats like we did. They must have got really cold waiting with you on the beach. I wonder why they were on the beach without coats in the first place – but I'm glad they were. You must have felt very grateful to them, because you licked them too, and then came back to me, smelling of sand and wet dog.

The best smells in the world.

Chapter Twenty-nine

Everything changed once we'd found you, Timmy.

We all came home and Mum rushed up to me and flung her arms around me.

'I'm so sorry, Anna. I'm so sorry,' she said and she started to cry, but someone else came and put her arms around Mum and me together.

'Come here, you poor loves,' said Aunty Helen. 'What an awful time you've been having.' She smelt great – all incensey and her earrings jangled and her jumper was soft and I didn't even mind her wavy hair getting in my face. 'Group hug!'

It was so lovely to see her, Timmy.

Aunty Helen said as soon as she heard my voicemail she tried to ring me back, and when she couldn't get an answer she just got straight into her car and drove to our house.

Everything got sorted – even the shopping,

which Aunty Helen managed to pack away or ask our neighbours to put in their freezers.

Emma and Lauren and Mohona were given a big towel and told to dry you off. We were both so hungry, weren't we? Aunty Helen made me a lovely hot toasted cheese sandwich and gave you your dinner. Gran was put on hot chocolate duty, and Mum and I sat next to each other on the sofa, not talking, not looking at each other, but happy to lean against each other. We were so tired. We watched as you tried to wriggle out from under the towel and eat more from your bowl. Gran handed round drinks. When Jack cried, Aunty Helen joggled him in a sling. He looked so cute and comfortable against all the patterns and colours of Aunty Helen's clothes. Everyone else talked and laughed, and Tom stood in the kitchen with his dad and watched the washing machine go round. Matt and Mohona's mum talked to Stinky Brown and his brother, and then Matt said he was going to take them home, but not before Gran made us give them three cheers. It was a bit embarrassing, but nobody really minded.

They were heroes, after all.

I was quite glad Matt did go, though, because

Gran had been talking loudly about how Frankie Santoro used to buy all her clothes from Mum's shop. And how Matt is a lovely boy and how they must have been a lovely couple. Honestly, Gran should write a magazine about celebrities.

You were still an awful mess and you smelt of seawater and sand, but you looked beautiful to me. You looked up and wagged your feathery tail. I could see it had a bit of seaweed in it, but I didn't care. I could definitely smell you, even with my nose, and there was no way I was going to let you be anywhere I couldn't see you.

Mum got up and went to find Gran in the kitchen, and Lauren, Emma and Mohona came over to the sofa.

'The Famous Five!' I said. 'There's five of us now at last.'

'I'm not sure about being famous, now we've missed the audition,' said Lauren.

'I'm going to be our manager – we will be,' said Emma confidently.

When everyone had gone home, I sat in the sitting room while you lay down and dreamed and twitched your paws and whimpered a little in your sleep. You must have been so scared before Stinky Brown and his brother found you.

'Shh, it's okay, Timmy – you're home. I'm here,' I said, stroking your damp head, and though you didn't wake up you must have heard my voice in your dream, because your tail started to wag.

I couldn't face going back up to my room and seeing what a mess I'd made, so I stayed on the sofa. Then Aunty Helen came and sat next to me.

'I'm sorry, Anna,' Aunty Helen said. 'Nobody realised quite how bad things had got. But it'll get better from now on – I promise. We had a good chat with Mohona's mum. She says there's no need to worry so much about Jack or sending him to America – he's doing much better than we thought and really it's your mum who isn't well after all the stress. So we've decided that she is going to have a proper rest, and I'm going to come here and help out when your dad goes away.' She gave me a big hug. 'Now why don't you round up Mum and Gran and see if they want another cup of something to drink.'

I looked down the hallway and saw that Mum was already in the kitchen. She said she didn't want anything, but she gave me a hug and a kiss good night. I couldn't see Gran. I walked up the stairs and noticed that the door to my room was properly open now. Oh no!

I walked in, worried that Gran would be standing there among all the mess, ready to tell me off.

But the chest of drawers was back in its normal place. The bedside light was on, and the floor was clear, and my shoes were back next to the bed, my bed made.

'Oh, Gran,' I said.

'Now, none of that, Anna,' said Gran, appearing at the door. She stood next to me and gave me a quick, awkward hug – nothing like the bear hug Aunty Helen gives, but it was amazing being hugged by Gran at all.

'You're a good girl, Anna. Now, into bed with you. I'll bring you up some hot chocolate. Oh, and take Timmy with you. You'll want him next to you tonight I expect. Timmy! Come here!'

I NEVER thought I'd hear Gran calling you upstairs.

And I think you were as surprised as me! You came up very slowly with your head slightly to one side, as if you thought it was a joke. Then you saw me in my room and rushed in and wagged your tail and sniffed everywhere before turning round a few times in a circle and then lying down.

When I turned back the duvet, my pyjamas were wrapped around a hot water bottle and when I put them on they were so warm.

'Thanks, Gran,' I said, sitting up in bed when she came in with a mug of hot chocolate. 'Thanks for tidying my room.'

Gran fussed around with my duvet, tucking it in, and said, without looking at me, 'Things will get better, Anna. Too many cooks spoil the broth. That's what the doctor said. Good night, sleep well. We're very proud of you, you know that?'

I'd never, ever heard Gran say that, ever.

'I love you, Gran,' I said.

'Right. Well, I want you to keep this bedroom as tidy as this in the future,' she said, sounding like the old Gran. 'And if you want a smelly old dog in your room you're going to have to brush him more and hoover, because he makes an awful mess. Look at the hair he has dropped already!' But she didn't sound as cross as her words, and when you thumped your tail on the floor and looked up at her, I'm sure she was trying not to smile.

It's Friday, Timmy.

Frankie Santoro
Day!

♫ 𝄞

Chapter Thirty

Aunty Helen brought me breakfast in bed and drove me to school in her really cool Beetle car. She's even got a little dreamcatcher hanging from the rear-view mirror. I want to be like her when I grow up.

I still felt a bit bad about Lauren not getting to sing for the TV people, but Emma said that she has a plan and that everything is going to work out. It didn't even bother her when Suzi and the others came into class and made a big thing about getting filmed yesterday. She just rolled her eyes and carried on sketching the new cover for Lauren's first album. Emma says it should be released on vinyl, as that's cooler than CDs.

Then Mrs Berlinski came and told us the two finalists had been chosen. The first was Ramon – Emma's brother! Not really a surprise because we all know he is brilliant and gorgeous and a sixth former.

'I'm really excited, though – as the second finalist is a Year 7 group *from this class,*' beamed Mrs Berlinski.

Suzi and the others smirked.

'I'm delighted to say that the second act is Steve Turnip and the Spiders. The judges thought they were very original and can't wait for Frankie to hear them today. So, well done and off you go, lads – make us proud!'

Wesley, Alex, Oliver and James looked stunned, but not as much as Suzi and the others. We couldn't stop smiling. I know that sounds mean but you have NO IDEA how annoying Suzi is. Well, you probably do, Timmy, as I go on about her so much. I'll stop now, I promise.

Then Frankie Santoro arrived at school. It was in English and we were supposed to be talking about *Oliver Twist*, but Miss Lacey let us all look out the window and watch. I think she was as keen to see a real-life superstar as we were. Three big black cars and a van with an aerial swept down the drive and lots of people got out carrying boxes and leads. Then the door of one of the black cars opened and someone got out, but we couldn't see much because whoever it was with some very tall security men and they all went in a group into the school. We all groaned and Miss Lacey said, 'Right, back to *Oliver Twist* until the bell rings,' but you could tell her heart wasn't in it and she would have quite liked to run down the stairs and get in to see Frankie Santoro before us, instead of having to stay with us, make us line up and walk quietly to the hall.

We were told to 'proceed in an orderly manner' and when we entered the hall there were cameramen there already and sound men with earphones and big, fluffy cloth sausages on sticks. I'd seen them on TV but I'd never seen them in real life before.

It was a bit intimidating, to be honest. I was glad my uniform was clean, but I was really aware that I had your hair on my skirt and freezing the tights hadn't worked as well as I thought it would because I had a big ladder on my left leg. I decided that I was glad we hadn't won the audition. We need more time to work on our image.

The senior choir was on stage ready to sing as Frankie went up the central aisle. Wesley, James, Alex and Oliver were on one side of the stage and Ramon was standing on the other with his guitar. Mr Parsons waved his hands about and told us to be quiet and Mrs Derbyshire, looking really fed up, made Rishi and Sam, who'd been playing air guitars and laughing, come out and stand with her at the side. Then they looked fed up too.

'I want you to give a BIG Bekesbourne High greeting to Frankie Santoro!' said Mr Parsons, and suddenly the doors of the back of the hall opened and the cameramen rushed down from the top to walk backwards filming Frankie Santoro and her backing band coming up the aisle and on to the stage as we clapped them. They all looked so cool, Timmy – the men were wearing flat caps and carrying drumsticks, a guitar and a saxophone, and she was dressed in a black and white Edwardian striped dress and a big black hat with ostrich plumes.

'It's from Buttons and Bows,' I whispered to the others. 'It was the dress from the window Matt wouldn't let us borrow.' I bet Suzi and her friends wouldn't be so snooty to me about 'old clothes' in the future.

So then we all sang 'He Ain't Heavy, He's My Brother' and I did my best *Songs of Praise* singing face and looked really interested and alert for Gran's sake.

Then Mr Parsons got up with the microphone.

'As you know, Frankie is an old girl of this school.'

Old girl! Imagine calling Frankie Santoro that. Mr Parsons can be so embarrassing.

'Sadly for me, Frankie was just before my time, but I've read up about her life, and she is a remarkable young woman. She isn't just an extremely talented musician, but she was absolutely heroic in the way she cared for her mother while she was still at school, so she is a role model for you in so many more ways than a normal pop star. And now she has come to launch her charity here!' He handed the microphone to her, practically bowing. 'We couldn't be more proud of you, Frankie. Welcome back!'

'Thank you, Mr Parsons and hello, Bekesbourne High!' she said.

We all cheered but she just smiled and waited.

'Thanks so much for having me, and thanks to the choir for your amazing singing! There's serious talent here, I can see. I can't wait to work with you as a school and get to know you better.'

Emma nudged Lauren. Maybe she hadn't missed her chance.

'I've come here to launch my charity, but I totally

don't want people to say I was heroic or saintly or something for being my mum's carer. I want to tell you that I loved my mum so, so much, but being a carer was the hardest time of my life. The song says 'he ain't heavy, he's my brother' – but I'm here to say that sometimes people's burdens are too heavy. I know I felt really alone when I was a teenager and often couldn't cope, and I seriously messed up my exams. It was music that saved me. My mum always loved to hear me sing, and my dad, who died when I was little, was a musician, so I've named my charity the Alice and Claudio Santoro Foundation. Its aim is to encourage music in schools. I want to provide opportunities for everyone, and I especially want to see if I can help young carers like me.'

She looked over to Kaz Baker. 'Okay – I believe you have chosen two acts to try out for our charity single?'

'Yes, we have chosen Steve Turnip and the Spiders,' announced Kaz, and Wesley, Oliver, James and Alex waved. They had put leather jackets on over their school shirts and looked much better than normal.

'Cool name!' said Frankie, smiling. 'And cool costumes!'

207

'And our other group is in fact a soloist. His name is Ramon and we think he has an amazing voice.

'Great! Let's hear you both, then,' said Frankie, taking a seat on the stage next to Kaz and Mr Parsons. The cameramen and the sound recordist positioned themselves at the front, their backs to us, and Kaz beckoned Ramon on.

Ramon sang a cover of Frankie's song 'Give Me Time'. He has such a gorgeous voice. I saw Priya standing up near the stage and she clapped him really loudly at the end.

Then it was Steve Turnip and the Spiders. It was amazing. Who knew Wesley was such a good guitarist? James and Alex just did chords but they were really good at dancing with their guitars. Oliver is a fantastic drummer. The problem was, they were all so loud! They chose Frankie's song 'Calling Out Your Name' and you couldn't hear any of the words. Wesley did a cool guitar solo, though, and James and Alex played their guitars and skidded across the stage on their knees, like rock stars. Ramon looked fantastic and sounded much better, but I have to say they were much more exciting. Everyone clapped at the end, and the judges put their heads together to decide. Frankie got up.

'Thank you SO much!' she said. 'You both were so different and you both had such strengths that we have decided we need Steve Turnip and the Spiders AND Ramon to combine.'

Wesley shouted, 'YES!' and then looked embarrassed as if he hadn't meant to do it out loud. Ramon looked happy but a bit unsure.

'Mrs Berlinski says she has been through the backing parts with both of you this morning,' said Frankie, 'so let's set up now and sing "Don't Put Out The Stars" – our first Santoro Foundation charity single – and maybe we'll sort out the balance of the Spiders' guitars a little too.'

'I think she means turn the volume down,' I said to Mohona.

'Good!' she whispered back. 'Do you think they could unplug them altogether?' Mohona is not into loud guitars.

The technicians came on stage and fiddled with the microphones and set up Frankie's band, and then, when the drums and the guitars and saxophone and singers were all in position, Frankie started singing the first verse.

'Well, I like Frankie Santoro, and I like her charity, and I liked the saxophone solo, but I didn't think much of the song,' said Emma as we were eating our sandwiches in the canteen. Aunty Helen had made me some really nice cheese salad ones. 'I think it's just as well you didn't have to sing it, Lauren. I feel sorry for Ramon. His songs are so much better. That's rubbish about stars dying through lack of love. They're already dead anyway – they died millions of years ago. And clouds don't put them out.'

'I think it's meant to be poetic, Emma,' said Mohona. She's better at English than Emma.

'Well, I think we can put on our own concert and write our own songs that make a lot more sense,' said Emma. 'So it's just as well Lauren didn't get linked with Frankie Santoro at this stage of her career. I just hope my brother can cope.'

Emma really makes Lauren laugh. It's funny because they hated each other and now I think they are going to be best friends. And I pity anyone who gives Lauren a hard time if Emma hears them now.

After assembly, Emma got Lauren to go and talk

to Mr Parsons about everything. It must have worked because Mrs White came to cover for chemistry in the afternoon and she was really nice to us and even smiled at Lauren. Miracles do happen.

We've got some great ideas for raising money for Frankie's charity:

1. Baking cakes.
2. Sponsored dog walk.

Pretty genius, eh, Timmy? Aunty Helen bought you a harness and it's much easier to walk you on that now.

3. Sponsored singalong.

But we mustn't over-tire Lauren's voice because our best idea is:

4. Have our own band concert at Emma's family cafe.

Chapter Thirty-one

I can't believe it! More dribbling! We really need to work on your table manners. Although this mushed up vegetable stuff does look a bit gross. I would probably spit it out too.

Look at Timmy, Jack. He's not as messy as you – and that's really saying something. And he doesn't blow raspberries! Though you really make me laugh when you do, Jack! You make everyone laugh.

You're six months old today and everyone says you're doing so well! Are you looking forward to your party? Dad has made an amazing cake already. Mum and Gran and Aunty Helen are getting the room ready now.

It's going to be great.

It's a good thing you two stayed at home with Aunty Helen last night for our concert. We were a bit loud. Aunty Helen heard us in the dress rehearsal and she said we were fantastic, though. And we were. It was such a good idea of Emma's.

Lauren and Ed were brilliant. After we got Mrs Berlinski to listen to Lauren singing she said she had a rare talent and put her name forward to the Santoro Foundation for support. Now they pay for her singing classes. Matt got talking to Ed the day he found you, Timmy. It turns out Ed is a carer too. He's only got his dad. It's really hard. Ed's dad is an alcoholic and nobody knew except Ed. So Ed's been looking after himself and his brother all the time. It's been awful for him.

But now Ed plays the drums in our band, and nobody calls him Stinky Brown any more because Frankie's charity has got help for his family and she has been paying for his drum lessons. He's really, really good. Frankie even says she will sponsor Lauren and Ed to go to music college, like she is going to do for Ramon, if they want to when they are older. But that won't be for ages yet and I'm glad. It's so much fun us all hanging around together. I'm never going to be brilliant, but my violin is much better now I can practise at home. Miss Green says I am making progress. You don't even cry when I play, Jack, and I notice you don't howl any more, Timmy. Thanks for the support, guys.

I LOVE being in the band so much. It was the best fun ever playing in the café. Ramon played too and we raised lots of money for Frankie's charity. Emma's dad was so chuffed when Frankie and Matt turned up too – they just slipped in at the back . . . together. Gran says she isn't surprised.

You caused a big sensation when Mum took you to the shop, Jack. Frankie was visiting Matt and she said you were the sweetest baby she'd ever seen, and you are . . . you really are. I love it now I can cuddle you. You are so soft and round and smiley and we can't stop passing you round and giving you hugs. I love being your big sister!

And, Timmy, I've found my homework that I read out in Mr O'Connell's class. It was weeks late, but he was fine about it. You can hear it too, Jack. It's about a hero.

My Hero

If a hero is someone who should be your role model, then mine is my dog, Timmy. He is fun and friendly and always there when I need him, and he gets on with all my friends and family. He is patient and kind and always, always looks for the best in people. I have never heard him growl, his tail is always wagging and he is the best listener ever. I love him. And he looks great in hats.

AUTHOR'S NOTE

I am a lot like Anna. Like Anna, when I was in Year 7 I fell in the luggage rack on the bus, and like Anna, I always seemed to be in a mess — one of my teachers really did describe me as a 'walking disaster'. I write a lot of lists, I like doodling, and I own a golden retriever dog I love very much whose name is Timmy.

The other reason I am like Anna is that I was a carer. This is why I wrote *Dog Ears*.

I cared for my mum for five years before she died, and even though I was an adult, with a supportive family, I found it very hard and overwhelming and isolating at times. I used to think that if I could find it so hard as an adult, how on earth did child carers cope? I read reports by the Children's Society about how many children were doing this most difficult job, and how it was affecting their school lives and happiness, and I wanted to write about this.

When I was an adult carer something wonderful happened. A person called Helen Neame contacted our GP surgery. She was training to be a psychotherapist — someone who is especially trained to listen to people and help them — and she asked if my doctors knew anyone who would benefit from having therapy from her whilst she trained. They knew I was very stressed and they recommended me. This meant that nearly every week whilst Helen trained, and after, when she had qualified, I had someone outside my family who was there to listen to me. She listened to me every week (and sometimes twice a week) when I told her about how tired I felt, or angry, or sad, or despairing or lonely, and she helped feel better about myself and got me get through this most difficult time of my life. I cannot thank her enough. This book is dedicated to her.

I hope that if you are a young carer you get the support you need. I want to keep telling everyone how special and hard the job is you are doing, and how we as adults must not ask you to take on more than you can cope with. This is not right. I think it is wonderful that organisations like the Children's Society have noticed and are listening to young carers, and I hope that the links at the back of this book will help you get the help you need. I hope that you get someone to listen to you like Anna, Lauren and Ed did, and that by following these links you get the practical and emotional help you deserve.

You're not alone.

YOUNG CARERS

A young carer is someone 18 or younger who
provides care and emotional support for a relative
with a condition, such as a disability, physical
or mental illness, or an addiction.

A BBC report in 2010 estimated that there are
around 700,000 young carers in the UK.

Research suggests that 1 in 12 of children at school
are young carers - that's roughly two in every class.

Children as young as 5 have been
identified as young carers.

Charities such as *The Children's Society* and *Carers
Trust* provide support to young carers and
to schools and communities in identifying
and helping young carers.

Links to these organisations and information on
how you can get in touch are on the page opposite.

INFORMATION AND SUPPORT

The Children's Society
www.youngcarer.com

www.childrenssociety.org.uk

Contact the supporter care team: 0300 303 7000

EMAIL: supportercare@childrenssociety.org.uk

Makewaves Young Carers in Focus social network:
www.makewav.es/ycif

Carers Trust
www.carers.org

Carers Trust online chat website for young carers:
babble.carers.org

Childline
www.childline.org.uk

TEL: 0800 1111

For more information on young carers, go to:
www.youngcarer.com/resources

www.carers.org/what-young-carer

ACKNOWLEDGEMENTS

Thank you to my wonderful agent, Anne Clark, who understood why I wrote *Dog Ears*, who encouraged me to contact the Children's Society when I was researching it, and who read and commented on my first efforts and made them better.

Thank you to the Children's Society for their encouragement to me whilst writing *Dog Ears*. Their work is so important and, sadly, so necessary.

Thank you to my amazing publisher, Catnip Books, and in particular my gifted editor Liz Bankes, who worked so hard on this with me, and the talented cover designer and illustrator Pip Johnson, who created the beautiful cover, designed the book inside and let me use my doodles! (I feel very excited and proud about this!) Thank you to Robert Snuggs, Pip with her marketing hat on, and the team at Bounce for all their support and hard work telling people about this book – I'm a very lucky author!

Thank you to Francesca Willis, who was in year 7 when I wrote *Dog Ears* and who came up with Anna's band's name!

Thank you so much to Ruth Washington for her love and support as a friend, and for sharing her experience as a Year 6 teacher at lovely Barham Primary School.

With thanks to and in memory of a great dog lover and supportive fellow writer, Linda Crammond of Anne Clark's Literary Agency.

Thank you to Judy Ayris, the Age UK Dementia Support nurse in Canterbury, who helped our family care for my mum. All carers need supporters like her. Thank you to Helen Neame, to whom this book is dedicated.

Thank you to my dear friends Katy Wilson and Virginia Moffatt for always encouraging me and getting me through my wobbles whilst writing *Dog Ears* and in life in general! I want to thank my lovely friend Jane Gleeson, who listened to me when I told her how much I wanted a dog, and helped me get my own Timmy, my first dog.

Thank you to my own teenagers, Joanna, Michael, Laura and Christina, who patiently put up with me asking them about school life, and were able to give me instant feedback as I wrote. Christina even told me all about the band name generator, which was a lot of fun to try. Thank you so much – I love you very much!

Thank you to all the friends and family who have listened to me during the years.

Most of all, I want to thank Graeme, the best husband in the world, who always loves and listens to me.

Anne Booth lives in Kent with her husband, four teenage children, two dogs and three hens. She has worked as a bookseller, a university lecturer and in a care home. She writes fiction for readers aged 9 and up about friends, families and the small but significant choices we all face every day, as well as younger fiction for 6+ and picture books.

Anne's powerful debut novel *Girl With a White Dog* was published by Catnip in March 2014.

Girl With a White Dog received outstanding reviews and has been nominated and shortlisted for numerous awards including the UKLA Book Award, The Carnegie Medal, The Little Rebels Children's Book Award and the Waterstone's Children's Book Prize 2015.

www.catnippublishing.co.uk
Twitter: @catnipbooks